"Slim, serious, and searching, *Hunting in America* revolves around some major topics right now: the experience of our inter-country relations, gun usage in our country, and the vacuous void at the center of one's quest for power and meaning in America."
　　　　—Julia Hass, *Lit Hub*'s "Most Anticipated Books of 2025"

"Sexy, witty, and spare, like an unexpected stranger with whom you might be persuaded to leave a party. Except the party's in middle America and involves guns."
　　　　—Elisa Albert, author of *Human Blues* and
　　　　The Snarling Girl and Other Essays

"Provocative . . . Told differently, the novel could be a classic noir, but Hakimi keeps the reader on their toes with the narrative's disarming obliqueness and ambiguity, all the way to the final crack of a gunshot. This tantalizes."　　　　—*Publishers Weekly*

"In this astonishing debut novel, Tehila Hakimi weaves a darkly seductive tale of alienation and desire and asks hard questions about the sacrifices made and challenges faced by women in a male-dominated workplace, revealing the violence inherent in our daily lives. Hakimi's protagonist straddles the thin line between reality and fantasy, between cultures and languages, between hunting and being hunted. Utterly gripping and chilling in its razor-sharp precision, *Hunting in America* will leave you breathless."
　　　　—Ayelet Tsabari, author of *The Art of Leaving* and
　　　　Songs for the Brokenhearted

Tehila Hakimi is a Jewish Book Council Award–winning fiction writer and poet. She was a participant in the 2018 Fulbright International Writing Program Fellowship at the University of Iowa, and is a recipient of the Israeli Prize for Emerging Poets by the Ministry of Culture as well as the 2015 Bernstein Prize for Literature. Hakimi's short prose and poems have been published in translation in *Asymptote*, *World Literature Today*, and *The Poetry Review*, among others. She was also awarded Israel's 2019 National Library's Pardes Scholarship for writers and the 2018 Levi Eshkol Memorial Prime Minister's Prize for Hebrew Writers.

Joanna Chen is a British-born writer and literary translator from Hebrew to English whose translations include Agi Mishol's *Less Like a Dove*, Yonatan Berg's *Frayed Light* (finalist for the National Jewish Book Awards), and Meir Shalev's *My Wild Garden*. Her own poetry and writing has appeared in *Poet Lore*, *Mantis*, the *Los Angeles Review of Books*, *Narratively*, and the *Washington Monthly*, among other publications. She teaches literary translation at the Helicon School of Poetry in Tel Aviv.

HUNTING IN AMERICA

A Novel

TEHILA HAKIMI

Translated by Joanna Chen

PENGUIN BOOKS

PENGUIN BOOKS
An imprint of Penguin Random House LLC
1745 Broadway, New York, NY 10019
penguinrandomhouse.com

Set in ITC Berkeley Oldstyle Pro
Designed by Sabrina Bowers

Library of Congress Cataloging-in-Publication Data
Names: Hakimi, Tehila author | Chen, Joanna (Translator) translator
Title: Hunting in America: a novel / Tehila Hakimi;
translated by Joanna Chen.
Other titles: Yariti be-Amerikah. English
Description: [New York]: Penguin Books, 2025.
Identifiers: LCCN 2024059772 (print) | LCCN 2024059773 (ebook) |
ISBN 9780143138662 trade paperback | ISBN 9780593512807 ebook
Subjects: LCGFT: Thrillers (Fiction) | Novels
Classification: LCC PJ5055.23.A38545 Y3713 2025 (print) |
LCC PJ5055.23.A38545 (ebook) | DDC [Fic]—dc23
LC record available at https://lccn.loc.gov/2024059772
LC ebook record available at https://lccn.loc.gov/2024059773

First published in Hebrew as יריתי באמריקה (*Shooting in America*) by
Achuzat Bayit Publishing House, Tel Aviv, Israel, 2023

Printed in the United States of America
1st Printing

The authorized representative in the EU for product safety and
compliance is Penguin Random House Ireland, Morrison Chambers,
32 Nassau Street, Dublin D02 YH68, Ireland, https://eu-contact.penguin.ie.

To my love

THE FIRST SHOT ——

1

The first time I went shooting in America I hit a tree. We'd been outdoors for a while, probably a few hours. The first shot hit a tree, but the next one whistled through the leaves. I stopped shooting, the animal fled, and everything went quiet.

When I raised my head from the gunsight, I noticed David and the others staring at me, and I was embarrassed. I left them where they stood and approached the tree. I searched for the bullet but couldn't find it. It must have penetrated the trunk. The scent of the earth was pungent and overpowered the acrid smell of the gunpowder, which dissipated into the air. I remained by the tree a few more moments.

We had left the office early that day, shortly after lunch. There had been an awkward conference call with Israeli management that morning. The information they offered was unclear, their messages mixed, and the conversation left everyone uneasy.

I was catching up on emails when David came into my office and asked if he was interrupting. He told me they'd decided to finish up for the day, and when I looked at him in confusion, he smiled and said he was going out to the field to shoot with some of the guys. "Would you like to join us?"

When I returned to where the others stood, David patted me on the back. I shuddered, feeling each of his fingers through my sweater. They were spread apart, like in yoga class when the instructor tells you to extend your fingers and toes like duck feet. David murmured something like "Way to go" in a somewhat perfunctory tone that nonetheless felt good. I usually didn't like it if someone offered encouragement when I was already doing my best—it had the opposite effect on me. I smiled and said it had been twenty years, maybe more, since I'd shot a gun. Until that moment I'd preferred to put behind me the fact that I had once handled firearms, but suddenly it came back. It just slipped out, I barely noticed.

2

I **thought I had a pretty good understanding of**
American etiquette long before that, but no amount
of TV, movies, email correspondence, or videoconferences with
American colleagues had prepared me. For starters, the daily
office routine was more tiring than what I was accustomed to
back in Israel. For an entire month, I found myself wandering
around feeling jet-lagged. This wasn't the usual fatigue of a
transatlantic flight, nor was I homesick. I didn't regret my decision to leave Israel. On the contrary, I arrived in the United
States with a sense of relief and anticipation.

During the first few weeks, my long workdays ended with a
pounding headache. Flashing an automatic smile every time
someone approached me became a habit. The smile was wide,
but not the kind that creates wrinkles. Convincing enough, although I didn't entirely recognize myself. It was the kind of

smile suitable for a profile picture on LinkedIn, or maybe a dating app.

I got to know David better during that first week. Every day, he dropped by my office to invite me to join the engineering team in the cafeteria for lunch breaks and to let me know what time they were meeting up. Besides David, I chatted a few times with Sean, a young guy I'd already corresponded with a little before I arrived in the United States. And there was Joan. We shared an office, and she was nice from the start.

The days were filled with constant stress. I made an effort to speak English without an accent. I wrote meticulous emails, trying to emulate the wordiness of my colleagues. It was Joan who'd tipped me off about the emails. One morning, before the daily grind began, she cornered me, closing the door to our office. She said she knew it wasn't deliberate, and I shouldn't be embarrassed—she had family in Israel and understood the mentality—but the direct tone of my emails might be misconstrued as aggressive. "They already have a boss," she concluded with a smile. Later that day she sent me an email with copious comments. She'd copied one of mine and attached it to a separate document with corrections. She opened brackets after every other sentence and explained how to rephrase it. Her explanations were detailed and mostly began with these words: "It would be even better to write this." In addition to her deletions and comments, she made sure to occasionally compliment me on a successful turn of phrase. When I thanked her for her help, she said it was her pleasure, that it was no big deal. "You're a quick learner. Soon you won't need me anymore," she added.

3

The second time I went shooting in America, David brought along two of his friends. It was a Saturday, and this time no one from the office joined us. Once again I was the only woman, but I was used to this. Most of the time I was the only woman on the team, the only woman in the meeting. Sometimes I was the only woman in the entire building.

David said we were going to drive further out, to a different area. They'd received an email from the local Fish and Wildlife authority with whom they were registered, inviting them to help reduce the number of deer. The idea was to shoot to kill but also to scare them off, to move them away from the most densely populated areas. "Like warning shots," I told David, who didn't seem to get it and threw me a suspicious look. On the way there, he said it would be good hunting practice for someone like me, who was just starting out. He explained there was usually a specified bag limit, but that licensed hunters had been repeatedly called on since the beginning of the season to help with the deer situation. I mostly kept quiet and listened carefully while he was talking, I wanted to get up to speed. At this stage I still didn't have my own rifle, so David lent me one of his. Most of my coworkers possessed firearms at home, some even kept a gun in the trunk. There were also a few who kept a small pistol in the glove compartment.

It was raining when we arrived, but this wasn't a problem. David said the rain would help us, that it would make it harder for the animals to feel our presence. "Under the cover of rain," I said, nodding knowingly. He looked at me weirdly again. We drove further along. The road narrowed into a dirt track, and David slowed down. After a while, he stopped the truck, turned to face us, and said, "Ready?" He didn't wait for an answer.

David led the way, I walked behind him, and the other two followed. After thirty or forty minutes, I heard the signal we had agreed on, a birdlike chirp, to indicate that an animal was close by. We froze. David subtly lifted and lowered the palm of his hand. This was the sign to hunker down. We sprawled on the ground.

When I saw the buck standing in front of me, it was in repose, barely moving. Now it was up to me. Before the others had time to exchange glances or determine which of us had a direct line of vision, I had already fired. One shot and then another. One to the torso and the other to the neck. A moment later the buck fell heavily to the ground.

We approached the dead buck, and David identified the points of impact. He looked carefully at the first point, bleeding at the center of the torso, and then he turned to me and said it was a beautiful hit. Afterward he pointed to the neck and said, "But not that one."

The three of them dragged the buck to the truck. First, they wrapped it in a kind of tarp and then covered it with thick material that David had tucked into his backpack earlier. Finally, they tied it up with rope. Everything happened fast, they were clearly skilled in this line of work. They took turns, two of them dragging it at a time. I followed slowly behind. All was quiet. During one of our pauses, David turned to me and said, "That's one hell of an animal you got yourself. Not bad for a first hit."

The buck landed in the spacious cargo bed, and the truck sank down. We drove back. After we had dropped off the others and it was just David and me, I apologized for moving so quickly, firing before a decision had been made. He was silent for a few moments, then said there was no need to apologize.

"I think you're a natural," he said, almost in a whisper.

We didn't talk on the way back to my place. When he pulled up beside the path leading to my house, David said he had a lot of work ahead of him: He had to take care of the animal, he had to take care of the meat. He said he would come pick me up later. As soon as I slammed the truck door, or even a split second before, he drove off. From where I stood, I could see the truck sagging under the deer's weight. The cargo bed almost touched the road.

4

Those first few weeks in America went by quickly.
I was busy figuring out how things worked in the
office and finding my way around the spacious house in which
I lived. I made no effort to keep in touch with friends back in
Israel. I spoke to my parents once a week, despite my mother's
nagging me to call more often. They let me be only after I explained that I was under a lot of pressure at work and that
weekends were a better time to talk. The atmosphere in the office was tense, but it wasn't clear why. Joan taught me everything I needed to know to navigate my way around the huge
building and avoid making tactical errors with my colleagues—
those I didn't know, and those I did. It was often tougher with
the ones I already knew; I was no longer a name on an email or
a face on a video call but a person in the flesh.

Sometime during those first few weeks, Joan suggested that
we go out for a drink together after work. She was a big-boned,

hefty woman, but when she drove her truck she somehow seemed smaller, almost my size. On the way to the bar, she asked me how I was doing, whether I had everything I needed in my new home, and whether they were taking good care of me. Her questions were not presumptuous, she didn't ask anything overly personal. When we got to the bar, I tried to resume our earlier conversation and asked about her family in Israel. When had she last visited them? Where did they live? "I'm not really in touch with them," she said. Joan ordered a beer, and I ordered the same. The beer was strong, and I didn't enjoy it. But when the barman suggested another round, I agreed right away and didn't wait to see if Joan was going to have another one too. When Joan said, "No thanks," I briefly considered canceling my order, but in the end I drank it down all at once. When we left, I was slightly buzzed.

As we drove back to the company parking lot to my car, Joan blurted out that she and her husband were trying to get pregnant. "We've been trying for a long time," she said. After we parted ways, I sat in my car until I was sober enough to drive home.

5

The new house was already fully furnished when
I moved in. The company had taken care of everything. Someone from Human Resources had been in touch with
me a few weeks before my relocation. She sent me photos of
couches, dining tables, rugs, and drapes, but I didn't respond in
time. When I entered the house for the first time, a heady smell
of paint hung in the air. Still, it looked nice and tidy, and everything was spotless. It wasn't until weeks later, when the smell of
fresh paint had worn off, that I began to notice a certain must-
iness.

One evening, as I was sitting in the living room, it occurred
to me that everything in the house had been chosen by another
woman. I had not picked out a single object or piece of furniture. That weekend, I went to an IKEA in a city some distance
from my house. I knew that something was missing, but I didn't
know exactly what. The trip to IKEA took two and a half hours

each way. Strangely, the store made me feel so at home that I almost forgot I was in America. I wandered around for a few hours until I reached the restaurant, which was located in a hall between the two main levels. I stood at the entrance for a few moments. Once inside, I couldn't decide what to order, so I took a few random plates of food: salmon with green beans, meatballs in sauce with mashed potatoes, and a hot dog with fries on the side. I ate a little of everything. It all tasted familiar, vaguely comforting. It was only after I removed my tray from the table and threw the leftovers into the trash that I realized I had left my shopping cart at the entrance to the restaurant. It was filled with bedding, a towel or two, and some kitchenware I thought I might need. I didn't go looking for it. Instead, I went out to the parking lot and drove home.

6

Sometime during my third month in America, Joan disappeared. At first I didn't ask questions. It didn't seem important. I assumed she was on vacation and had forgotten to tell me, or perhaps she was on sick leave. All of her personal items were still there, including her computer. After a while, her desk was emptied and nothing remained of her in the office. When I asked David what had happened, it took him a moment to figure out who I was talking about. Joan had had very few interactions with our team. On rare occasions she would reply to emails from clients, because she worked in the commercial department. David and I worked in project management, and we interacted with a lot of other departments within the company. A few days later, at our weekly meeting, David told me that he'd inquired about Joan and learned that she was on unpaid leave for personal reasons. I assumed it was because of her attempt to get pregnant, but I said nothing about this to David. A week or two later, I went down to the Human Resources department. I wanted to get her phone number, I thought maybe I would call her. When I reached the door, I changed my mind. If she'd wanted to keep in touch, she would have left a note on my desk or sent an email. As it happened, there was no one in Human Resources anyway.

Around that same time a sense of insecurity began gnawing at me. There was a lot of gossip spreading from company head-quarters in Israel. Unverified reports of organizational changes, rumors about closing or downsizing several branch offices. I tried to calculate the chances that my own business division would be eliminated. I convinced myself that the chance was low; in the short time since my arrival several major projects had been added, and we were inundated with work. I couldn't imagine the company letting us go. These thoughts disturbed me mostly when I was alone at home, after work.

I spent my first few weekends doing nothing. The hours flew by, and on Monday mornings when I returned to work, the weekend was erased entirely from my memory. On the short drive to work I practiced what to say if someone asked me how my weekend was and what I'd done. I prepared answers I could extract quickly, grocery shopping in Costco, reorganizing the basement, washing clothes. The only two weekends I'd gone out were the Saturday I went hunting with David and the Saturday I went to IKEA.

After a few consecutive weekends of idleness, I decided to take up running again. It had been a long time since I had done this regularly. I didn't enjoy using a treadmill, but the weather, which was turning chilly, prevented me from running outside. I joined a nearby gym, and very early one Saturday morning I went there for the first time. I chose a treadmill that looked out over unending green, similar to the view from my new house. The gym was quiet, almost empty. I started out slowly and gradually increased my pace. My body felt cumbersome, my muscles were rusty. I wasn't running fast, but even so I felt I wouldn't be able to keep it up for more than a few minutes. Then my phone began vibrating. It was Tal, my boss from Israel. He'd called a few times that week, and every time I tried calling him back it went straight to voicemail: "I'm not available right now but will get back to you soon, thank you." Now I deliberated whether to pick up. I didn't want to sound out of breath, but the phone continued vibrating. His call went to voicemail and immediately after he called me again. I stopped the treadmill and went outside.

Tal apologized for disturbing my weekend and announced he was arriving in America at the beginning of next week. He was landing Sunday afternoon and wanted to have dinner with me that same evening. The phone call was very brief and businesslike. He did not specify the reason for his visit. When I went back inside, I increased the pace, my legs flew above the belt, my body felt lighter. On the treadmill next to me was a hefty-looking guy who hadn't been there before. He was already running hard and breathing heavily. I felt drops of his sweat spatter on my arms and legs. I stopped the treadmill. I got off so fast I almost lost my balance. In the locker room it took me a short while to find the locker where I had stored my belongings. Everything looked the same. After a quick shower I went out to the car and realized I'd forgotten to dry my hair. The cold air froze my head. Trembling, I ran to the car, holding the keys in my outstretched hand. As soon as I got in, I turned up the heat as high as it would go. It took several minutes before the trembling stopped.

7

Tal's flight was delayed, and dinner was canceled. In the end we met up at the office on Monday morning. After a quick round of niceties we went into one of the conference rooms. He spoke fast—at first he said one thing, and then he said another. He contradicted himself again and again. He said he believed it would take time for management to release a formal decision regarding the US unit. He repeatedly told me there was nothing to worry about, that they intended to "keep" me. He said the changes would be far-reaching, but that in any case, as far as they were concerned, I still belonged to the Israeli headquarters. "You have nothing to worry about," he insisted, stressing I was part of the budget, and the way things were going it could take two or three years until management decided what to do about employee relocation in the United States. The palm of his hand struck the table lightly when he said "United States." When I asked him what the precise decision was, he cut me off and said that the point of his visit was damage control. He wanted people to keep on working, "and as far as you're concerned," he emphasized, "it's business as usual." Finally, he said I should take care of my own interests. When he was done, he went quiet and looked at me for a long moment. I told him I wasn't worried at all. We left the small conference room and went over to the main one. Everybody was there, sitting around the table, including David.

David began presenting the quarterly review, but Tal interrupted him and asked to say a few words. "I want to clear the air," he said in a polished American accent. "There's a bunch of rumors going around and it's scaring the shit out of everyone." Then he said that the American branch office was the company's most significant one to date, one that consistently maintained quarterly goals, way above the average of all the others. The entire time he made eye contact with everyone sitting around the table but me. He concluded his speech with a commitment and said that as long as he was part of this company, the American office would neither be downsized nor eliminated—it would be expanded.

After he finished, Tal handed things over to David, who began to go over the presentation, slide by slide. Someone switched off the light, and the room was illuminated by the bluish light of the projector. I stared at each slide. Quarterly review, goals and performance, future projects, current projects, and two to three slides on special projects. When the presentation was over, we all went out for lunch.

8

A couple of days after Tal left, I woke up in the middle of the night and discovered I had a few unanswered calls. It was one of my friends from Israel. We hadn't spoken in months. I looked at my watch and calculated that it was already noon in Israel. I clicked on a news app in Hebrew. Nothing catastrophic had happened. I browsed through our WhatsApp exchange and saw that the last time we were in touch was a few months before I left. Maybe she wasn't even aware that I was no longer in Israel, that I'd left. I tried to remember if I told her, if I wrote her about it. I put the phone aside. I assumed she'd called me in error.

Sleep evaded me. The house was silent. I lay in bed for a while, but no matter what I did, I couldn't get back to sleep. Eventually I realized it wasn't going to happen, so I went downstairs to my office. I switched on the computer and searched the web: *Introduction to deer hunting.*

I clicked play on the first video that came up. "The first thing to do," the man said, "is to check with your local Fish and Wildlife agency about what can be hunted in your area. And then, of course, you've got to know where the animals are." I fast-forwarded. He was detailing the areas in which deer like to roam, and the areas they pass through. "At the edge of the woods," he said. Deer like the edge of the woods. I followed the points on a map that appeared on the screen, thin tracks circling trees. It was important to uncover travel corridors. It was important to move very slow, step by step, heel-to-toe and again heel-to-toe. "If you're stalking and you're on the ground, it should take you sixty seconds to get up off the ground."

I moved on to the next video. After that finished, I watched another one. Then it was morning. I went upstairs to take a shower before leaving for work. I practiced the hunting walk, heel-to-toe, heel-to-toe across the rug in the hallway. The floorboards creaked under my feet.

9

The third time I went shooting in America, there was heavy fog in the area. It was a Monday, and I was on vacation from work because of a holiday or some kind of a memorial day, I'm not sure which. This time it was just the two of us, David and me. He said he'd texted a few friends, but none of them joined us. We agreed to set out early, and David picked me up from my place at six in the morning. He suggested that we avoid the fog and go a bit further afield. That's how he spoke, in general terms, almost never specific. The area where we hunted was the ground, no matter where we were, the deer was an animal, and the birds were all birds. Whether we ate chicken or turkey, or went out shooting pheasants, David called them birds.

We stopped on the way for a break. When I got back from the restroom, there was a cup of coffee and a plate of food on one side of the table for David, and the same waiting for me on the other side. David had gone ahead and decided what to order for me. It was a typical American breakfast: eggs, bacon, butter, a grilled tomato, the tasteless kind that doesn't improve when cooked.

We drove in silence, and as David had hoped, the farther we went the better the weather conditions became. Finally, the fog cleared. He parked the truck, and before we removed the equipment from the back seat, he said it was important to start practicing the silence we would need to adopt during the hunt. He gripped my shoulder with his hand. "This time we'll keep quiet while walking along," he said. I nodded and turned to open the door, but something stopped me, he still gripped my left shoulder. "And you're not going to shoot until I give you the signal, be patient this time," he said.

We walked into the grounds. The clusters of trees grew increasingly dense, an unending continuum. We kept going and David did not turn around, not even once. I walked behind him quietly with the obedience of a soldier. While doing so, I practiced the heel-to-toe, heel-to-toe hunting walk—until David froze in place. He crouched, and I did the same. Finally, he lay down on the ground, thrusting his arms in front of him, holding the rifle. After some minutes he rearranged himself on the ground, and then lay there, motionless. I stretched out on the ground like him, I did everything he did. "Monkey see, monkey do," as my mom used to say when I did something that seemed dumb to her, something I'd learned elsewhere, in kindergarten or school, or from a friend. Especially if I cursed, because there was no cursing at home. I remembered her words right there in the woods but managed to suppress my laughter. I bit my lower lip so hard I almost broke the skin. I lay there, my body flat to the ground, motionless. I still couldn't see anything. I couldn't see any animals in my line of fire, neither to the right nor to the left. We lay there for a while, until David turned his head toward me. He beckoned me to crawl toward him. I began advancing slowly on my belly, commando style. As I drew closer, he signaled me with his elbow to hunker down to his left, so I did just that. My right boot was practically touching his left one. We remained in this position on the damp ground, lying as if in ambush, until I suddenly heard a movement, but before I had time to figure out where it was coming from, David fired a shot. I didn't move, I lay there close to the ground until he signaled me. Then we got up.

10

A week later David invited me to join him and some of our colleagues in a bar after work. Most of my colleagues, like David, were older than me. Almost everyone was married and most wore wedding rings. David wasn't wearing his wedding ring, and I didn't know for sure, but I guessed he had kids. Before he went over to the jukebox, he asked if there was anything in particular I'd like to hear. I said I wasn't sure what they had there, but that I trusted him. The bar seemed familiar, it was the kind of bar I could have imagined before even stepping into it. David took his time, and when I looked around the bar, I saw him standing by the jukebox talking to a woman I didn't know. In the background, Tom Petty's "Into the Great Wide Open" was playing. I'd thought about that song when I'd arrived, when a great expanse of green appeared through the window of the airplane before landing. I didn't see the face of the woman talking to him, but I watched as her mane of red hair took on hues of pink, purple, or blue, depending on the light radiating from the jukebox. As they talked, David smiled broadly and laughed out loud, in fact they were both laughing. That was the first time I ever saw him laugh like that, and I wondered if one day I'd make him laugh like that as well. Toward the end of the evening, as we sat together at the bar, he suddenly said he wanted us to move forward, that we should buy me a gun of my own.

That evening I continued my online training in hunting. I watched a few YouTube videos and fell asleep. The next morning, I woke up early. The open laptop lay beside me on the bed. While I was asleep the videos kept playing on mute, one after the other. On the screen was the red gunsight of a rifle, trained on a group of three deer. I watched the video and a few seconds later the gunsight shook. One of the deer collapsed and crumpled to the ground.

11

A few months earlier, back at the airport, my transfer flight was delayed again and again. I began to think I would never get there. I had planned the trip so that I would have a few days to settle in before my first week at work. Every time I checked the departure board, my flight was pushed back by another hour, another three hours. I wandered around the terminal, I walked by all the stores, the majority were closed. I continued roaming around until I got to the business lounge, the one you need a gold card for, or a platinum one. I thought to try my luck although I wasn't a member in either club. When I entered, I found myself by the sleeping pods. This was the first time I'd ever come across them. The pods were located against a wall, metal structures painted green, modern cabins with a spaceship appearance. I peeked inside one and wondered whether there were closed-circuit cameras inside. After a brief deliberation I chose number two. I swiped my credit card, and the door opened. On the window of the door hung a roller blind. I pulled it down as far as it would go. From the inside, the pod looked like a small cabin on a ship. I wasn't sure I'd be able to fall asleep there. People were walking past my pod, they were probably curious, and from time to time I heard fingers knocking at the window. Dull knocks, almost imperceptible. It didn't bother me, I knew I would have done the exact same thing. A few hours later I woke up in the pod. Luckily, I had set the alarm on my phone. I slept soundly, out of time. According to the latest update on the departure board, there were two hours remaining before my connecting flight. I gathered up my belongings: laptop case, jacket, carry-on bag. I splashed water on my face and dried it with the paper towels provided. The pod contained almost everything necessary, in miniature. I looked at myself in the small mirror and fixed my hair, arranging it first to the right and then to the left. I combed it through with my fingers. The left side had more white hair, but this no longer bothered me. I released the blind and it rolled up noisily and stopped with a click. Then I pressed the green button that opened the door. The door slid open and the lights flickered softly in farewell. I stood outside the pod and watched as the door closed. I remained standing there, looking through the window into the pod. I watched the bed changing its own sheets, like a conveyor belt, the sheet and blanket moving along together. A small door opened above the pillow and a metal arm switched the pillow for a new one. The lights went out.

When I got to the departure board, written next to my flight were the words *Final Call*.

12

At first glance, the gun shop looked like a regular camping store. On the first floor were different brands of hiking apparel: waterproof jackets, fleeces, hats, scarves, and endless varieties of thermal socks. At the other end of the floor was the shoe department, with long shelves stacked with footwear according to size. The place was so huge, I lost David soon after we entered.

I found the gun department on the second floor. There were hundreds of firearms, probably more, maybe even thousands. They were arranged according to size, maybe according to brand too. I surveyed the entire floor, wondering where to begin. In the automatic rifle section, I found a short-barreled M16 that looked similar to the one I'd used in the army. It had a price tag—seven hundred dollars. I took it off the shelf. It was heavier than I remembered. I passed it back and forth between my hands, testing its weight.

I pressed the pin located next to the grip with my right thumb. The pin slotted through to the other side, and I pulled it out with two fingers. The rifle opened and then folded. I removed the charging handle together with the bolt carrier and held them in one hand. Everything happened like clockwork. It was like muscle memory, in one smooth motion, a swift sequence of automatic actions. I returned the parts to the rifle until they clicked back in place. It was only then that I noticed David, holding a shopping basket with contents I couldn't see. He stood a few yards away, watching me.

In addition to automatic firearms, the store stocked hundreds of different hunting rifles. There were very long ones with wooden stocks, or a combination of wood and metal, or plastic and metal. There were pistols, air guns, even bows and arrows, vintage and heftier state-of-the-art models. There was also a wide variety of bullets, displayed behind glass panes like in a jewelry store.

On the way to the customer service desk, I passed displays of camouflage suits and hunting blinds. In the window of one of these tentlike hunting blinds, the little blond head of a toddler appeared. I watched as the toddler lost his balance and fell on his butt whenever he tried pulling himself up to the window. A lanky blond guy, the toddler's father, stood outside the hunting blind, laughing at his son's antics. Interspersed throughout the store were video screens with commercials for electronic systems that calculated the distance from the target, connecting to the rifle's gunsight and trigger and collecting real-time data. After a minimal number of uses, the system was able to calculate various shooting statistics, including the chance of hitting a given target. My eyes were drawn to several tall ladders in the center of the store, leaning against equally tall, dense structures that resembled trees. These were tree stands, designed to camouflage a hunter lying in wait for an approaching animal. There were also shooting targets I had never seen before. The ones I knew from my IDF service were made of cardboard; the American ones were made of a rigid plastic material. They came in the shapes and sizes of various animals. I saw deer targets in different sizes, and turkey targets too. There were even small rabbit targets. The biggest target I saw was a bear target. There were panda and wild boar targets. There was almost always a marker on the deer targets, slightly below the center of the torso, indicating the location of crucial internal organs. An elliptical marker indicated the lungs, heart, and liver.

Above the marker on one of the targets were the words DEER QUARTERING AWAY. When I asked David what this meant, if it was perhaps the deer's center of mass, he looked at me blankly. Then he explained that it was the most efficient area to aim for when bowhunting deer.

"This is the single most effective kill zone," he said, adding that the marker was designed to define areas of the body that were ethically accepted to aim at. "Most hunters want to kill the animal for meat or for caping, but a decent hunter doesn't want to injure it for nothing or cause it unnecessary suffering."

When I got to the service desk, I asked the sales assistant which rifles he recommended for deer hunting. He swung around to the huge display of rifles on the back wall and removed one of them. I held the rifle in my hands for a few moments. It was a bolt-action rifle. I wanted to ask if it was available with a magazine, but I couldn't think of the word in English. I got stuck midsentence and had to gesticulate with three fingers how it went in and out.

"Do you mean the magazine?"

"Yes, that's exactly what I mean, like an M16. I had a rifle like that in the army."

"Thank you for your service," he promptly said and added that he had automatic rifles too.

I told him that I did not serve in the US military, and I wasn't from here.

"Serving in the military is always good," he said. He took another rifle down, said perhaps this would suit me, and placed it on the counter between us.

Before going back to the ground floor to look for David so I could register the rifle in his name, I held the 7mm Remington rifle I'd selected. It had a beautiful wooden stock and looked overall more elegant than any of the other rifles the sales assistant offered me. I aimed it toward the floor and then at a point on the wall facing me, I pressed the stock of the rifle against the crick of my shoulder and trained my right eye on the gunsight. It went blurry for a moment and flickered. I closed my right eye and opened it again and the crosshairs sharpened. Then I pulled the trigger.

13

The fourth time I went shooting in America almost ended in disaster.

We were lying on the ground in silence, waiting to see if there would be any movement. We had set out early that morning. There were four of us—we were joined by two of David's friends who were visiting from the South. We were on David's property, and it was very cold. I dressed well: I wore another layer over my thermal clothing to conserve body heat.

That morning I got a message from David with a list of instructions:

Wear thermal clothing today, no need for thick gloves, possible light rain in the afternoon, pack your storm suit.

When we entered the area, we were bundled up from head to toe. I recognized David, but I had trouble telling his two friends apart. After a slow walk we reached a spot that looked out over an open space. I positioned myself beside David. We lay there for a while until David signaled me, and a moment later I glimpsed a movement with my free eye, the left one. My right eye was trained on the gunsight the whole time. David's friend, lying to my left, also noticed. I saw him tensing up. Right from the start there was something weird about the movement, but in any case, my finger slid toward the trigger guard and fluttered over the trigger. But I didn't squeeze it, not yet. I focused my right eye on the gunsight, but the visual field of my left eye was blurred. A moment later I heard barking, and three people appeared, dressed in camouflage gear. I quickly removed my finger from the trigger guard and secured the rifle. Without thinking about it too hard, I angled the rifle toward the treetops and unloaded it. David and the other two turned their heads toward me in one quick motion, and when I looked at David I saw an expression on his face I had not yet encountered—fear and confusion. We got to our feet, together, all four of us.

David yelled to the people in the camouflage gear and beckoned them over to us. When they were close enough, he moved toward them, signaling us to stay put.

On the way back I asked David if he knew any of them, and he said no. "This isn't the first time my property's been invaded," he concluded dryly. When I asked what could be done in such a case, he said it was a minor criminal offense, with either a fine or up to a month in jail, but since no damage was done, there was no reason to make a big deal out of it. He stressed the word *damage*. I nodded and said we were really lucky. "We sure were," he replied.

When I got home, I switched on my computer and typed in the search bar: *Can you shoot someone who trespasses on your property?* The answers that appeared said that if a trespasser committed a violent crime, armed force could be used if needed, but it emphasized that "this does not authorize the shooting of any unwanted person passing through the curtilage in your possession."

14

The fifth time I went shooting in America, we were on the grounds behind David's house, and we shot at targets, not animals. It was a Saturday, and he sent me a text early that morning: *We're going out for a bit of shooting, Miriam wants you to come.*

This was the first time Miriam's name had come up in our conversations. When I arrived at their place the table was already set for breakfast, three plates and cutlery. Although I had lost my appetite by then, I joined them. There was no need to cause unnecessary embarrassment or offend Miriam. My stomach had shrunk after a few months in the US. Everything tasted the same—coffee, bread, vegetables, spices; only meat had a taste. Usually I skipped one meal a day, sometimes two. My appetite gradually disappeared as the weeks went by.

Even though this was our first encounter, Miriam and I acted as if we had already met, as if we already knew each other. There was something gentle and refined about her. Her straight gray hair was pulled back and gathered at the nape of her neck, her face was delicate and lovely, her green eyes were very bright, and she looked much younger than she really was. She made a salad especially for me because she had heard from David that I always looked for salad in the company cafeteria and was always disappointed with the options. Later she said that David mentioned that I had served in the IDF. The letters rolled over her tongue as she said them. They sounded like an acronym for a medical procedure. For a moment I imagined she had said IVF. I gave her my automatic response, that everyone had to do military service in Israel, and that mine was more than twenty years ago. Obviously this wasn't accurate, but I didn't have the patience to explain that not everyone did it, or why. She said it was impressive and maybe that's where I got my shooting instinct. When I glanced at David, I saw the glimmer of a smile cross his face. He hardly spoke during the meal.

After breakfast, I sat there awhile longer and had another cup of coffee while David and Miriam did the dishes. They stood with their backs to me, working in perfect coordination, barely exchanging a word. David scraped the dishes and rinsed them; Miriam dried the dishes and stacked them on the countertop. Every so often Miriam's body drew almost imperceptibly toward David's and gently rubbed against him. For a moment they appeared as one body that had split and reconnected like a machine driving some essential movement. The water flowed from the faucet the whole time. David turned it off only when all the dishes were done. I heard my father's voice in my head: "Folks over there don't have a water shortage, they've got water coming out of their ears."

When we went outside, Miriam led the way. I strode along behind her and David followed me. We dressed warmly, although this time we didn't wear camouflage suits, and everything was less bulky. On the way we passed a small lake on their property. It was a clear day, and the weather forecast did not predict rain. David had taken some empty beer cans, and we walked along until we reached an open space.

About fifty yards from where we stopped were several tree stumps. Miriam pointed to them and said those were our targets. While David went to place the cans on the tree stumps, I warmed my hands, removing my gloves and rubbing my palms together. David came back and said we could begin.

"Everyone keep to your own firing line."

I crouched down, the beer can flew off the stump at my first shot. I didn't wait for the other two. They each fired a shot, first David and then Miriam. They both hit their beer cans right away.

"You can go down there and replace the cans if you like," Miriam said, "but everyone keep to your own firing line." David continued loading bullets and shooting although he had already knocked all the cans off his tree stump. I said I'd rather not, and added that where I came from, it happened quite a lot that people shot each other in the back. Miriam looked at me and laughed uneasily.

15

The sixth time I went shooting in America I didn't miss a single shot. Miriam came with us again. She was a good shot, thorough and deliberate. She took her time getting into position, steadying herself, taking aim. Miriam showed interest in me, she asked questions and occasionally placed a gentle, almost nonchalant hand on my shoulder while talking to me.

|ılıılıul

The seventh time I went shooting in America we went back to the tree stumps. Miriam wasn't feeling good and stayed home. We began setting up a few beer cans, and David suddenly asked if I remembered the first time I shot a gun.

"My first time ever?"

David nodded.

I told him I couldn't really remember, it was probably at the shooting range during basic training. I had no clear recollection of the first time, and anyway I never shot people or living things, only cardboard targets. Sometimes the targets were decorated with balloons.

We continued shooting. I missed one beer can and it flew up into the air and ricocheted above the tree stumps. After two or three more rounds, we took a break and ate the sandwiches Miriam had made for us. While we were eating, David said that Miriam was in one of her moods again, it happened a lot at the beginning of winter. "She finds it hard to adjust," he muttered quietly, and that was all he said. Then we began shooting from further away. There was a dull thud when a bullet hit the target, and a long whistle when the bullet missed. On the way back to the house, we passed the lake again. As we approached it David slowed down, then stopped and stared across the icy water. We turned to go and he murmured softly, so softly that perhaps he didn't want me to hear, "This was Tom's favorite place."

16

The eighth time I went shooting in America it was very cold. Temperatures plummeted that week. It was my first winter there; it was freezing outside and snowing heavily. According to weather reports, snowfall at the beginning of that winter was way above average, a record amount of snow for two decades.

When we were still in the truck, David handed me a smartwatch with a body temperature sensor. It was Miriam's. I asked if she might need it, but he said no, she'd gone to her sister's. Afterward he told me she always went away in the winter, but he didn't elaborate any further. He patiently explained to me that the most important thing was to let him know if my body temperature dropped below the green line. Miriam's watch also monitored heart rate.

The snow felt good under my feet, like walking on the moon. We calculated the depth of the snow as we walked, compressing and hardening beneath the soles of our boots. Light snow began falling as we made our way to the lookout point, but it made no difference to me, I was well protected by my storm suit. Under the suit I wore several thin layers and another thick one. We walked along for a while, I glanced at the watch, my temperature was normal—above the green line. David stopped and we hunkered down, the snow had tapered off by now. Contrary to guidelines I'd come across on YouTube, David didn't look for tracks. I figured he knew the area well and didn't need to. We lay there in the snow for some time, and then David turned his head toward me and signaled for me to check my temperature. It was still above the green line.

David had first watch. He removed his thick gloves and wore only the lightweight ones. After fifteen minutes he gave me a sign and we switched. Almost an hour passed, and before the end of my second shift, David gestured to me that we were packing up. We walked some more, until David came to a halt. We hunkered down, and not long after that, we saw them moving toward us. There were two of them, side by side. It was my turn, and I watched them slowly advancing, entering my line of fire, but something prevented me from squeezing the trigger. I couldn't focus.

It wasn't my fingers. It was cold, but my fingers weren't numb. By the time I managed to steady the rifle, both animals had exited my line of fire. I was dizzy as I lowered the rifle to the ground. It was as if David were swirling around me, the bare trees, the snow, all that whiteness. It only stopped when I heard him say, "Okay, let's take a break."

We didn't speak during our lunch break; in fact, we'd hardly exchanged a word all day. David reached for the thermos and poured me a cup of coffee. After he finished his sandwich, he resealed the thermos and returned it to his backpack. As we got to our feet to start out again, he asked me out of nowhere, "Were you ever married?"

17

About a month into my first winter, sometime after that first snowstorm, there was a lull in the bad weather. The sun even appeared for a few days. Around that time I received an important phone call from Tal, my manager in Israel. He caught me just as I was leaving for work. He didn't beat around the bush, he told me right away he was quitting. He said he didn't know if this came as a surprise to me, because of course there had been warning signs.

Only after showing interest in his new job and the company he was joining did I ask what management intended to do about his departure, if he thought they'd be replacing him or if they were counting on another reorganizational shuffle. Tal interrupted me and said this was exactly why he'd called, that it was crucial we spoke about that too, irrespective of his own departure. "You need to be on the ball," he said. He spoke without pausing, he said the CEO was not sure whether my position was necessary, that he had heard the CEO say on several occasions that he thought my position should be removed from the budget of Israeli headquarters. He said that the CEO would prefer returning me to Israel, that it was only a matter of time, and that he didn't know what position they would offer me in Israel, if any. I asked what exactly he meant by that, and my voice cracked. I cleared my throat and repeated the question. My voice sounded weak and broken. He kept on talking, he said the CEO didn't get the importance of my role, that none of them got it. His tone intensified. I said I didn't understand. What did they have against me? Ever since I arrived in the US all my projects had been progressing well, and there were several new ones. But he didn't listen, he kept on talking. When he asked if I was still there, I looked at the phone and saw I had accidently pressed the mute button. I didn't say much after that, just that I understood and thanks so much for the update.

At the end of the conversation, he repeated his words, "You need to be on the ball." After we hung up, I remained on the couch. I was shaking all over. I waited for the trembling to stop, but it didn't. I ran through all kinds of scenarios in my head. I knew the CEO would need to come update the team on the projected changes.

I went to the bathroom and splashed warm water on my face again and again. When I looked in the mirror, I barely recognized myself. "You have nothing to worry about," I told myself out loud. I watched the water streaming over my hands, I heard that sentence three more times, the third time in a whisper so thin I wasn't even sure where the voice was coming from.

18

At work I tried to project business as usual. I did this until about ten in the morning, when David came by my office. I told him we needed to discuss several issues and half an hour later we met in the conference room. I closed the door and cut to the chase. I told him about Tal's phone call, about his leaving, I stressed it was off the record, and David nodded his head. I said the CEO would be coming for a visit and that he wasn't convinced I was necessary to the company. I repeated everything Tal said.

David looked at me and after a few moments of silence said I had nothing to worry about. He slid his hand across the table toward me, almost reaching me, almost touching, but then stopped and rapped his fingers on the table, like he was knocking on a door, and repeated, "You have nothing to worry about."

David changed the subject and began to talk about the new project. He wanted to go over some edits he'd made to a requirements document for one of our clients. Back at my desk, I noticed my hands were shaking again. I thought perhaps I'd overdone it with the coffee and I thrust my hands between my thighs and the seat of the chair, one on each side. I was alone— no one had been assigned to my office space since Joan left. I closed the door and somehow managed to calm down.

I met David at lunchtime in the cafeteria, he was standing by the vending machine. As we made our way to the tables, he said a heavy storm was expected in our area and we wouldn't be able to go out. It took me a second to understand he was talking about hunting.

"But if you like, we can drive a little further out," he added.

When we got to the tables, he said we'd speak later. I sat down and he turned away, he had a working lunch with one of the engineers.

Later, he sent me a few text messages.

So what do you say? Do you want to hunt in another area?

I replied that I'd be glad to, and then he wrote me a second text: *If you like, we can leave this afternoon and stay the night somewhere along the way, and tomorrow morning we'll set out bright and early.*

Let me know when we're leaving, I replied.

Half an hour later he texted: *Let's leave at six thirty.*

I'll be there.

MEAT——

1

When I got into David's truck, he was holding the phone to his ear. "Speak to her, she wants a word with you." He handed me the phone. I heard Miriam say "Hi," and before I had a chance to respond she said, "Take care of him, okay?" and laughed. "For sure," I said, "always," and I asked how she was and whether she was having a good vacation. She laughed again and said, "Vacation!" and added that she was in good hands and that was the main thing. Then she said she didn't want to delay us any longer and that I should take care of David and tell him to drive safe. She hung up before I had time to say goodbye. I handed him back the phone and repeated her words. He put the phone in his pocket. It was stormy outside, but after driving for a couple of hours we seemed to have escaped the worst of it. David exited the highway and pulled up to a hotel. The hotel looked new, or perhaps it had undergone extensive remodeling. A sign at the entrance to the parking lot said: POOL OPEN 24/7.

David insisted on carrying my bag into the hotel. He gave the front desk clerk our reservation number—we each had our own room. He handed me the key card and said it would be a while before dinner. Then he turned back to the clerk and asked when Joe's Tavern closed, and he said they served food until nine in the evening, even nine thirty. "It's Friday today, they're flexible," he added. As we walked toward the elevators, I told David I'd like to check out the pool before dinner. Since we had time on our hands, it would be a nice way to freshen up after the long drive. We got into the elevator and David pressed the buttons for floors three and five, and when we got to the third floor he exited the elevator, and I went on up to the fifth floor.

I stripped quickly. I took my swimsuit out, something I bought in one of the airports on my way to the US, a sports bikini I'd been too tired to try on at the time. The mirror in the room was huge, there were signs of cellulite on my thighs, but even so my body looked in better shape than usual. It was probably the running, or maybe the long treks we did on hunting expeditions, or my lack of appetite.

The pool was small, around forty feet long, with a circular hot tub at one end. It was empty and, until David came, I was alone there. He undressed by the side of the pool and carefully folded his clothes and placed them on one of the chairs. I watched from a distance, there was a calmness in his movements. It's always embarrassing, the first time you see someone from work in a swimsuit, whether a man or a woman. I'd experienced this in Israel, mostly at team-building events or the annual company retreat. But in David's case, his half-naked body didn't embarrass me at all, perhaps it was the slow movements, the quiet confidence. The closer he drew toward me, the younger he looked. He was thin and muscular, his chest as smooth as a young boy's. On the left-hand side was a long scar that traversed his body from abdomen to armpit. He gestured to me with one hand, and I moved to the hot tub. It was hard to see him through the warm water and steam. I closed my eyes, directed jets of water to my back and neck. My body was tense and sore. I sighed inwardly. After a while, David joined me in the hot tub. "Great idea, the pool," he said, plunging into the bubbling water. Locks of his silvery hair glittered through the foamy water, his legs almost touched my knees. We remained like this for a while, and then I stood up and exited the hot tub, making sure my breasts had not escaped the confines of the bikini top since it was not a perfect fit. I helped myself to a towel from the cart and wrapped it tightly around my body. Then I took a robe and wore it over the towel. Meanwhile, David stepped out of the hot tub, and we walked over to the elevators together. Once in the elevator, I pressed three and five. But when the elevator came to a halt on the third floor, David didn't move. I said nothing and the doors closed, the elevator went up to the fifth floor, and David waited for me to exit first. He walked behind me, down the hallway to my room. I opened the door with my key card but neither of us went in.

"I just want to stay with you a little longer," he said. "I just want to look."

When I asked about Miriam, he just shrugged and looked away.

I closed the door behind us.

2

The room was warm and comfortable. They must have turned up the heat. I removed the robe and towel and stood there in my bikini. David remained by the door. I took the swivel chair next to the writing desk and rolled it along the floor as far as the bathroom door, then gestured for him to sit. I went into the bathroom and saw David in the mirror, sitting on the swivel chair. I opened the shower curtain completely, as far as the wall, and removed my bikini bottom and then the top. I hung them up on a hook fixed to the door.

I got into the bathtub and let the water run from the lower faucet. When the water warmed up, I used the showerhead instead. I glanced across the room at David. He sat there without saying a word, his face impassive. He didn't move, he just sat there looking at me. I began showering in warm water and gradually raised the temperature until it was piping hot. I closed my eyes. Water dripped from my body and sprayed onto the floor, the bathroom filled up with steam. I washed my hair and soaped my breasts and belly. My nipples hardened. I could barely make out David through the steam, everything blurred. He was still sitting there. When I had washed most of the soap from my body, he stood up, took down two towels from the rack, and placed them by the sink. Then he exited the bathroom. I turned off the faucet and carefully climbed out of the bathtub. I took the towels, wrapping one around my body. They were warm. Then I heard him unlock the door. "I'll be waiting for you downstairs," he said, and I heard the door close. I noticed he'd returned the swivel chair to its place by the writing table. I locked the door from the inside.

I lay down on the huge bed, loosened the towel, and wiped my thighs dry on it. I spread my legs out on the bed and began to stroke myself, first with the towel and then with my fingers, first slowly, and then faster, rhythmically, and after that I slowed down again, shut my eyes, pressed my head against the pillow, and I saw him again, his discerning gaze, this time not blurred, but very clear. I inserted one finger and then another, after a few minutes I shuddered and came, one fist gripping the towel.

3

The ninth time I went shooting in America, I hit a deer, a young one. "That's a very young animal," David said as we stood over it, examining the wound. On video clips I watched on YouTube, they referred to very young deer as "bambis." David referred to them all as "animals." I preferred it that way, hunting bambis seemed too cruel to me. David dragged it all the way to the truck. Halfway back, I asked if he needed help, I didn't want him to do all the hard work himself, even a young deer is heavy. He said there was no need, he was doing fine. He tied up the animal with rope. I held the rifles and the two backpacks. Before tying it up, he wrapped the animal in a plastic sheet that he took from his backpack. He secured the plastic sheet with another rope, several knots around the neck, and a few more around the legs. The animal bled into the snow. David let it bleed. As we stood by its side, waiting, David explained it would be easier to drag this way, and easier to handle the flesh later. More blood dripped onto the snow from the plastic sheet as David began again to drag the animal along, all the way to the truck. I walked behind him, following the trail of blood.

Halfway back, we came across a group of four hunters. They were headed in the opposite direction but nonetheless offered to help David drag the animal to the parking lot. At first he refused, but they were insistent, and he eventually agreed. When we got back to the truck, David thanked them, and they exchanged contacts. He invited them to come hunting on his property if they were ever in the area and felt like it, he said there was plenty for everyone and they should just let him know.

The journey back was tough—the closer we got the harsher the wind became, snow didn't stop falling. David drove slowly. I offered to switch places a few times on the way, but he said it was fine, he had no problem driving in these conditions. When I looked into the distance it was difficult to distinguish between earth and sky, the horizon was completely obscured. Everything was white.

When we stopped to eat, it was early evening, I ordered a hamburger and vegetable soup as a starter, which turned out to be as bland as its description. David ordered half a chicken with roast potatoes on the side, he sucked the chicken bones the way my mother always did, and, just like her, when he finished sucking the bones, he went on to gnaw their insides.

He stopped his truck outside my house just before midnight.

I asked if he wanted help getting the animal out of the truck bed but he said there was no need, he intended to leave the animal overnight.

"It's all the same to the animal, it can't run away."

The air outside was freezing. I grabbed my belongings from the back seat and ran inside, shivering with cold.

The house was freezing too, for some reason the central heating was not on. I switched it on and immediately called David. He answered right away, before I even heard the dial tone.

"The house is freezing, the heat stopped working," I said, and before I had time to add anything else, he said he was coming to pick me up.

4

When I woke up the next morning in David and Miriam's guest room, I saw he had placed my clothes on a table by the door. The clothes were clean—he had washed and dried them. I dressed, washed my face, and went downstairs. David was in the kitchen making breakfast, the smell of frying hung in the air. As we sat down to eat, he told me he had invited a few people from work. "They're coming around four."

He said we had time to work on the animal and then on the meat; it would take us a few hours, we should start at noon.

When I suggested we go buy liquor David was glad and said it was usually Miriam who reminded him of stuff like that, he had a habit of forgetting things, aside from the meat. On the way to the liquor store, we stopped by my house to check if the heat was working. At the entrance to the liquor store David took my hand and, still holding it, steered me through the aisles. We bought beer, bottles of red wine, and two handles of whiskey.

On our way back, I asked David when Miriam was returning. He didn't reply, although I was sure he heard me. I didn't ask again. Once home, David went out to the storage shed in the yard and returned with two folded coveralls. He handed them to me and went into one of the rooms off the kitchen and took out two small heaters. We walked out onto the driveway, half of which had been converted into a spacious shed, where we had dragged the animal. It was heavy, and David set the pace like a tug-of-war game, "One, two, three, and PULL!" he repeated, and every time we pulled, we groaned audibly under the weight.

He positioned the two heaters in the center of the shed and switched them on. Then he left the room, and when he came back he was holding a bottle of bourbon in one hand and two glasses with ice, clinking against each other, in the other hand. He poured bourbon into each glass and offered me one.

I waited to see what David would do next. He handed me a folding knife and took another one for himself. He flipped open his knife, and I followed his example. He slit the knots around the animal's neck, and I slit the ones around its legs. Together we unwrapped the plastic sheet from around the animal's body. David crossed over to the other side of the shed and dragged back a tall, massive contraption, a kind of hoist of welded metal rods. He beckoned me over and I helped him drag the animal to the hoist. He tied two ropes to its hind legs and tightened them. We made sure the knots were secure, and we lifted the animal by pulling on the ropes. David put one chair on each side of the hoist and then climbed onto one of them. Once up, he turned to face me, signaling me to climb onto the second chair. We positioned the animal with its head hanging down, facing the concrete floor. David dragged two heavy weights from the corner of the room and positioned them on the legs of the hoist. He poured another glass of bourbon and gestured me to come close. "Miriam won't be back anytime soon," he said, a moment after beginning to skin the animal. Later he explained that she usually stayed at her sister's the entire winter. All the while, I did exactly what he did, I drew long lines with the knife, I tried to penetrate the flesh without cutting too deeply. After a few overly deep incisions I stopped, and David continued. I watched him, he worked slowly and methodically, he cut long lines down the animal. I retreated, took a step back, I took another two or three steps back, and then a few more, until I reached the table and sat down on it. It took him a minute to notice I wasn't there. David turned his head toward me, the open blade in his hand, he did not leave the animal's side. I told him I wanted to watch, I wanted to see how he did it. David turned back to the animal but shifted a little to the right so as not to obstruct my view. He continued skinning the animal, and I sat up very straight on the table, straining my body in order to see better. I heard him breathing. At first it was barely perceptible, then it became heavier, and when he had almost finished skinning the animal, he turned in my direction again and I saw he was sweating. I heard the click of the knife as he folded it, and then he said he would tell me what to do to finish up work on the animal.

In the end we transferred what remained of the hanging animal to the table. David spread a thick plastic sheet over the table, and we laid the animal out. He brought a few bowls and knives from the kitchen. We put the good cuts in the bowls. The unusable parts, the excess skin, cartilage, and other inedible pieces, we dropped into two large bags.

5

The tenth time I went shooting in America Miriam had not yet returned from her winter visit to her sister. That same morning David had left me a voice message. He called me while I was at the gym. I didn't hear the phone ringing. I checked my voicemail, and right after the beep, I heard him breathing heavily and then there was a click as the call disconnected.

I called him back and it went straight to voicemail. I decided to go over to his house, and when I got there, I knocked on the door but no one answered. I went inside—the door was not locked—but he wasn't there, not in the living room or the kitchen, nor was he upstairs.

I waited for him in the living room, and after a while he walked in holding a rifle in each hand. A thick blanket was slung over his shoulder. He suggested we wait a little until the weather improved, meanwhile he said we could work on the rifles, they needed thorough cleaning. He spread the blanket out on the rug and placed the two rifles on it. I picked up one of the rifles and in one swift motion I made sure it wasn't loaded. I aimed it at the floor. I disassembled it by first opening the gunstock, then folding the rifle. I held the barrel of the rifle in one hand and the bolt carrier slipped out into my other hand. David cleaned the other rifle and from time to time looked up to see what I was doing. I arranged all the components on the blanket and cleaned them one by one. After cleaning everything thoroughly I began working on the exterior of the rifle. I polished the metal and cleaned the wood with a damp cloth. When I finished cleaning and reassembling the rifle, David helped me get to my feet on the rug. We stood close to each other for a few moments, until David's phone rang. When he answered, he was still standing very close to me. "Hi," I heard Miriam's voice. As I moved away, I heard Miriam asking if I was with him. "Yes, she's here," he replied, and afterward there was a pause and neither of them said anything. Even after I moved away, I could still hear her voice clearly. "Great," she said. "I hope you're not going out hunting." David told her that we'd wanted to, but the weather had turned nasty. "I fixed us coffee and now we're cleaning the rifles. Don't worry, if it keeps up like this, we won't go out today," he said. After that, I couldn't hear Miriam. Before he ended the call, he told her to look after herself, and then he repeated his words: "Do me a favor, look after yourself."

6

When we left his house that Saturday, David made me swear I wouldn't tell Miriam. When I asked him what he was talking about, he said I mustn't tell her we went out hunting in the stormy weather. Before we left, David went to Miriam's closet and brought me a thermal shirt. The shirt was a little small for me, but I wore it anyway. We left via the back door, crossing over the yard. I followed him to the far edge of the yard. David pointed to the trees and said I should aim for the tree on the left. We each had five bullets. He said he didn't want Miriam to see the shots, I should try to aim high so it would be out of her field of vision. I crouched down, but when my knee met the snow, it sank down and I lost my grip.

Snow fell incessantly. David fired a bullet that hit a tree, and immediately afterward a large chunk of ice broke and fell to the ground. He bent down and picked up the ejected cartridge. Snow fell the entire morning, inducing a heavy silence on everything but the shots we fired. I waited and did not shoot, I was waiting for him, I wanted us to shoot together. We stood close to each other, and David took a deep breath. After releasing the air from his lungs, he fired another bullet. I took aim, got a better grip on the ground so that the snow supported my boots on either side. I aligned the butt of the rifle to my shoulder and adjusted the angle of my arm. I inhaled deeply and then exhaled. I waited for him to shoot another round. After a few moments came the deep breath I was waiting for. I released my first bullet precisely when he did, the second and third too. We fired in perfect unison. David ran out of bullets, and I fired my last two haphazardly. The first bullet hit one of the laden branches, I watched the snow falling from the treetop. The final bullet whistled through the air.

I spent what remained of the weekend at home, I didn't plan anything. I checked my inbox late Sunday evening. Only then did I see the two emails sent by Dan, the CEO. In the first email he wrote he was in the US and wanted to meet me first thing Monday morning. In the second, he asked to confirm the time of our meeting.

7

At an early stage in the meeting with Dan, I realized they were looking for a way to get rid of me. At first he went around in circles with all kinds of talk about organizational restructuring. He used words like *probably*, *maybe*, *apparently*. But the bottom line was that they wanted to terminate my position. He spoke as if he were reading a script: "I need you to understand, we're seriously considering terminating your position." As he spoke, his eyes shifted from me to the table and back again. His speech alternated between first person singular and plural. From time to time, he referenced the organizational consultant, repeating that everything was coordinated with her. I remained silent while he was talking, either way it was impossible to get a word in. "Your position has become dispensable, redundant," he said. He added that many company departments were overstaffed. When I asked him if the organizational consultant had ever visited the US office, if she had ever spoken to any of the directors or employees, he squirmed uncomfortably in his seat. I said that I didn't know if he was up to speed with the details of my contract, but they couldn't fire me because I was under contract for a minimum of three years. I was on the verge of tears and hated the sound of my voice as it exited my throat, shaking. He said he was familiar with the contract, and they were interested in offering me a more significant position at company headquarters in Israel. "This is precisely why I'm here, we have a number of options for you." I wanted to slap him across the face. The room smelled bad. When he stood up to pour himself another cup of coffee, I noticed he was sweating profusely. A wet ring had spread over his back, and I could see his undershirt beneath his button-up. I felt like hurling a chair at him. Afterward he said it had taken him a while to appreciate that the industry was undergoing changes. He added that this change, like other proposed changes, would move the company forward. "We want you to be part of this change, we need you to take us to the next level," he said. He added that, after intensive work alongside a consultant, they'd come to the conclusion that there were positions within the company, both at headquarters and offsite, that were redundant. "It has nothing to do with your performance," he said. "We want to keep you." At this point he stopped talking, leaned back in his chair, and finished his coffee in noisy gulps.

"That's all very nice, but you should have thought about this before signing the contract," I said. As I got to my feet and started walking toward the door, he opened his mouth to say something, but I cut him off right away and made it clear that the only reason I agreed to relocate to the US was because the position was for a minimum of three years. If he, or his organizational consultant, or the board of directors, expected me to throw my life and career to the wind, to jump and go back to Israel, they could forget about it because it wasn't going to happen. "You don't have a concrete offer, and this is not a fair game," I said as I opened the door to leave. His forehead furrowed angrily, his cheeks reddened, and he opened his mouth to say something, but I had already left the room.

8

I went directly to the restroom, entered a stall, and locked the door. I tried to catch my breath, I thought I was going to throw up.

I came to my senses quickly, and from then on things moved fast.

"Go back to your desk right now. You have no idea what they're capable of. They may block access to your computer. Print whatever you need. You've got half an hour," I heard my own voice, still shaking. I left the restroom.

I went to my office, smiling automatically at everyone I passed. I opened computer files and printed them. I printed all my paychecks. I printed out time sheets. I printed all the email correspondence I'd ever received from the CEO, including my own replies. I printed out all the employee evaluations. These were all saved on my computer and the company portal. I printed a photo of me and the current CEO shaking hands when I received the outstanding employee award. I printed another photo of me and the former CEO shaking hands when I received the outstanding young manager award. This photo was much older, taken at least six years earlier. The printer churned out page after page. I printed my first employment contract. I printed the updated version of my old employment contract and my new employment contract, the one I signed before leaving for the US. I printed all correspondence regarding the conditions of my relocation to the US. I printed all correspondence with the head of Human Resources. I printed correspondence with Tal, who had already left the company. In addition, I sent each document as an attachment to my personal email address. I sorted through all the printed pages on my desk. By the time I heard a knock on the door, everything was organized in manila envelopes in my bag. Even my breathing had somehow returned to normal: air entered, air exited.

It was David at the door. The second after he entered my office, he said that Dan had informed him they were considering terminating his position. His conversation with Dan lasted almost an hour. He told me that for the first half hour Dan didn't stop praising him, and then he explained the situation to him. "They asked me to stay until the end of the year," he said. When I asked him what that meant, he said he didn't really know because it was all off the record, and he mentioned early retirement with good conditions. "I don't think they know what they're doing," he said.

I told him they want to eliminate my position as well, but that the CEO had assured me they had several options available to me in Israel. "A promotion," I said. "But I don't believe a word of it."

9

Just before the lunch break, David asked if I'd like to go eat at his place. "Miriam got back yesterday," he said. "I'm sure she'd love to see you," he added offhandedly. But I wanted to return to my desk as quickly as possible, because I wasn't done with Dan. "I'm not done yet," I told David.

We went out to a nearby diner. Although it was crowded and noisy, we were served quickly. David seemed lost in thought. I ordered the all-day breakfast. Carbs, proteins, oil and butter, whatever. The main advantage of diners like this was the coffee, as watered-down and tasteless as anywhere else, but with limitless refills. After the waitress had refreshed my cup two or three times, I refused more. My nerves were already jittery. Over lunch I realized that the main issue at hand was my contract. "What are you planning to do? Are you planning on making an announcement to the whole team? Are you going to call a meeting?" David finished chewing a mouthful of toast, swallowed, and said he was waiting to hear from Dan what his options were. He spat out the word *Dan*. Meanwhile I ran through all the lines I was going to say to the CEO: *You'll be hearing from my lawyer. You'll be receiving an official response through my lawyer.* Yes, that sounded more like it. David fell silent and looked at me. I was so wrapped up in myself, it took me a moment to react. "Yes, I get it. We need to find out what their decision is, and act later." David nodded in assent. I told him that in any event, unless I say otherwise, he mustn't tell anyone where things stood with me, not even Miriam. My face must have taken on a serious expression because so did David's. I said he had to swear he wouldn't tell. "Please, you have to swear you won't tell anyone," I repeated.

"You have my word," he said, and took the last piece of toast, spreading it with butter and jam. Then he wolfed down the toast in three bites without leaving a crumb.

10

The meeting with the CEO gave me no rest. That evening at home I read through my employment contract three times. After reading it, I wasn't entirely sure I had a case. That same evening, I wrote my first email to my lawyer. I'd heard about her a few years ago from a friend who was involved in a lawsuit against his former employer. She specialized in labor law, and I managed to find her after a few cross-references on Facebook. My Facebook account hadn't been active for a long time, and I had to reactivate it. After I located her website, I deactivated my account again. Then I wrote her a short, concise email. I informed her of my situation, my relocation, and the company's intention to eliminate my position and recall me to Israel. I stressed that the contract, in particular the addendum I signed before leaving for the United States, was supposed to protect me if my relocation was revoked. I requested a phone consultation. I attached my entire employment contract to the email.

The next day I caught the CEO briefly. He was meeting one-on-one with all the middle managers, one meeting after another. Around noon I burst into the conference room where he had been holed up all morning. "When did you say we were meeting next?" I fired at him in Hebrew as soon as I opened the door. I didn't even register who he was sitting with. We set it for eight o'clock the next morning. When I left the room, I restrained myself from slamming the door. I closed it softly but gripped the handle hard and yanked it upward instead of down. I gripped it so hard I thought it was going to break in my hands.

Back home that evening I prepared myself for the meeting by making a list of all the important points I wanted to cover. There were seven points in total. I read them out loud several times in a calm and composed tone, attempting to memorize them. I repeated the last point like a mantra: "And most importantly, keep your cool."

As I went upstairs, I inhaled and exhaled deeply, as if I were working out at the gym, but I couldn't steady myself. I stripped in the bedroom and, on the way to the bathroom, paused for a moment to look at myself in the hallway mirror. My body was caving inward, continuing its slow contraction toward the bones.

I had one foot inside the bathroom when the doorbell rang. At first I thought I had imagined it. I didn't even know there was a doorbell. It was the first time someone had rung it. For a moment I thought it was a kind of internal wakeup call. But the doorbell rang again and then there was a third short ring. I put on a robe and went downstairs. When I reached the door, I peeked through the peephole.

It was David.

HUNT——

1

We drove for hours. The road was monotonous and the light outside was gloomy. I sat in the passenger seat, dozing on and off the entire way. Whenever I opened my eyes all I saw was snow. At one of our stops along the way, I moved into the back seat and fell asleep. When we finally arrived at the house, I woke up, but sleeping in the truck had exhausted me. I stayed in the truck and David went inside to switch on the heat. A few minutes later he returned. He said it would be better to stay in the truck while the house warmed up. I curled up under a comforter David brought me.

When I woke up, David was looking at me in the rearview mirror.

"This is the first time I've ever run away from home," I said, abashed.

David laughed. Apparently it wasn't his first time.

———

The situation at work was at a standstill. We'd heard nothing since our last meeting with the CEO. They didn't tell David anything about his position, but they emailed me as soon as they received the letter from my lawyer. The email was sent by the administrative department of Human Resources and the CEO was cc'd. I was advised that I had a lot of vacation days and should use them by the end of the year. The email advised me to take a three-week vacation, effective immediately.

We were both deep in thought, I was worried about my job, and David kept quiet. I figured he was anxious about what they might offer him. When I asked him what he thought, he told me he had said nothing to Miriam about what happened at the beginning of winter. I wasn't sure what he meant, but I didn't ask him anything else because I didn't want to intrude. Later he said it might open old wounds: "I decided it would be better not to tell her anything," he concluded. The last thing he said confused me, but I didn't respond. I had no idea what he was referring to.

2

On our first night in the vacation home David of-fered to sleep on the couch in the living room so that I could sleep in the bedroom. When I said he could sleep with me upstairs, he didn't react, but when I went to bed that night he followed me up the stairs. The bedroom was cozy. David took out clean sheets from his bag and we made the bed together. The wind whistled outside the window, it was pitch-dark outside. When I looked at my face in the bathroom mirror, my eyes seemed tired, dark circles weighed them down. I was gray, rusty at the edges, my skin metallic. I washed my face with warm water and pinched my cheeks. I pulled my hair back for a moment and examined myself in the mirror. There was even more white hair. I applied moisturizer I found there, prob-ably Miriam's. When I went back to the bedroom David was standing there in his underpants by the bed, as if waiting for a sign. I got undressed and remained in my underwear and tank top. Then I got into bed and David followed. I lay there, my back to him. We lay there in silence for a while, the wind picked up, whistling with greater intensity, a storm was apparently brewing. Shortly after that I heard him breathing, his breaths gradually becoming longer and deeper.

That night I awoke to the sound of screaming. I opened my eyes and saw that David was awake too. At first I thought it was David, or perhaps the wind had hurled something at one of the windows. When I asked him what happened, he said I'd been screaming. He asked if everything was okay, and when I said yes, he went off to the kitchen to fetch a glass of water.

As soon as he came back into the bedroom, I knew what was going to happen. David groaned whenever my body pushed against his. Deeper and deeper. I wanted to be sure he was all the way inside. He groaned louder with every movement, and I didn't stop, his eyes were wide-open. I kept going, intensifying my movements until I felt him releasing, until he came. It was over quickly. I continued pushing against him, and then lay back.

3

The eleventh time I went shooting in America, I hit an animal. David hit one too. This was on the first day of our hunting expedition. On the way to the hunting grounds, David told me that he had improved his technique back in the days when hunting was severely limited. That was when he devoted his time out in the field to perfecting his aim. Sometimes he went a whole season without shooting a single bullet. He would lie in wait for the animals for hours, or watch them from a distance, tracking their tranquil movements. Sometimes he would crouch down and take aim at the target, he even squeezed the trigger without there being a single bullet in the barrel, just for practice. During those times he saved his quota until the end of the season, at which time he shot live ammunition and usually hit his target. Once he reached his quota, he explained, the adrenaline went down, and this was why he waited until the end of the season, so that when he finally shot live bullets, he did so with utter precision.

We left the first animal, the one David shot, on the hunting grounds, but David suggested we take the second one back to his house. It was a buck. When I told him I preferred to keep on hunting and that I had no desire to eat the animal, he looked at me blankly. I said he could do whatever he liked, but I wasn't going to eat that meat. The air was frozen when we got back to the parking lot, the snow had stopped falling but the skies were gray. It was clear that a storm was approaching. That evening I wrote my lawyer saying that I wanted to explore another direction, assuming Israeli labor law applied to my contract, as we'd discussed earlier. I asked what would happen if I was pregnant and informed my employer before receiving an official letter of dismissal. At the end of the email, I stressed that I was not yet sure I was pregnant.

4

When I returned to the living room David was sitting on the couch, there were two glasses on the table in front of him, and one was empty. The other glass was filled with bourbon, next to it stood the bottle. I had avoided drinks like this before moving to the US, but the cold weather and the overall vibe affected my drinking habits. Each time I tried a different type of local bourbon. I was open to the idea that every decade had its own drinks. The drinks I enjoyed in my twenties were not the drinks I enjoyed in my thirties, nor were they the drinks I enjoyed nearing forty. With time I grew accustomed to the robust taste of bourbon, deep and throaty with a sweet and sometimes spicy finish. Preferably on the rocks.

I sat down on the couch next to David, who was engrossed in a book. He continued reading, and I came to the conclusion that I had one more day of ovulation, assuming my calculations were correct. We'd had sex in the morning as well.

I resolved to limit my alcohol consumption. I drank slowly, sometimes I merely lifted the glass to my lips. After a while, David said he needed to make a call. Miriam hadn't been in touch for a few days, and he was concerned. He went upstairs to call her. He looked distracted but I didn't pay too much attention, not then, I wasn't about to pry. I opened the book I had brought with me.

It was a book I found on David and Miriam's bookshelf when I slept in their guest room. David said most of the books belonged to Miriam and I should help myself. He also said there was no need to return the books because Miriam intended to donate them either to the public library or to the local high school library. David preferred thrillers and didn't have patience for the books Miriam liked. "They are too heavy," he said, "the kind that put you to sleep after a couple of pages." I had brought *Little Tales of Misogyny* with me, a collection of short stories by Patricia Highsmith. In "The Hand," one of the first stories in the collection, a guy wants to ask for the hand of the girl he wants to marry. He turns to her father, who gives him his daughter's left hand in a box. The guy is deeply shocked by this horrifying turn of events and buries the hand in his backyard after kissing it one last time. The story ends with the young man behind bars, lamenting the part he unwittingly played in this awful crime. It was a terrible mistake to ask the father for the girl's hand, but when he finally confesses to his jailers and asks for forgiveness, one of them says to him, what exactly are you apologizing for, I also asked for the hand of the woman I loved. The guy feels he has lost his mind and stops eating. Eventually he dies, weak and skeletal in a prison bed, his face turned to the wall.

David came downstairs just as I was finishing the story. I was laughing out loud, and as David walked toward me, I noticed he was pale. I asked if he was feeling okay, but instead of answering me, he asked what I was reading. I told him about the severed hand and the guy who lost his mind and died, his face turned to the wall. He smiled halfheartedly and fixed his gaze on the other side of the room.

"We'll leave at the crack of dawn tomorrow morning," he said. "I want us to go even further out. The local Fish and Wildlife agency issued a warning that the day after tomorrow a bad storm's coming our way. We'd best get hunting while we can." David helped himself to another glass of bourbon. He was about to pour me a shot too, but I covered my glass with my hand. He downed the contents of his glass in one gulp and poured himself another one.

5

The twelfth time I went shooting in America, I was on target again. I shot only one bullet, and it hit what David referred to as the "safe zone." In my YouTube tutorials, too, this was defined as the best target area. I began to be more aware of the ethical code. The safe zone covered the lungs, liver, and heart. "If you aim for this zone," I repeated David's words to myself, "one shot is enough."

We slowly made our way back to the truck. David had difficulty dragging the animal and almost gave up. I was glad he refused my help; while hunting I'd completely forgotten I might be pregnant. The clock was ticking; all the clocks were ticking. In less than two weeks I was supposed to get a response from the CEO. I was also waiting to hear from the lawyer, who still hadn't answered my email. And my period would be due.

After we put the animal in the truck, David said he thought

he might cape the animal for mounting on the wall. "It's been a good while since I did that," he said.

In the truck on the way back, I thought about that one shot. The recoil of the rifle no longer caused me pain, I didn't feel anything at all. The muscles in my right shoulder had strengthened, and the layers of clothing helped absorb the blow. Only the sound remained the same, the explosion as the bullet struck followed by a long whistle.

David was mostly silent on the homeward journey and then he blurted out that Miriam was angry with him. When I asked what he was talking about, he said she'd found out about our shooting during the storm, at the edge of the yard. "We were dumb enough to leave the bullet casing," he muttered in suppressed anger, his lower lip trembling. "She went for a walk and came across the casing, just lying there, where we'd been shooting." I didn't understand what the big deal was because we'd all practiced shooting there on Saturdays before winter began, just a twenty-minute walk away. I didn't say anything, I didn't want to get involved. I tried changing the subject and asked if he planned to stop at the supermarket to pick up a few things before the storm set in. Finally, I decided to react: "Don't worry about it. By the time you get home, she won't be mad at you anymore."

"It doesn't matter, nothing matters anymore," he muttered.

As we were washing the dishes that evening, David said out

of nowhere that he died there, in the yard: "Tom, our son, that's how he died, a stray bullet."

I took a step toward him.

"When we went out the back to clean our guns, we didn't know he was there. Miriam was sure the babysitter was with him in the front yard. It was one stray bullet in the wrong direction. A bullet that should never have been fired. An accident." He stood there, his face to the sink. I took another step toward him and then stopped. He continued. "She says I've betrayed her. That I've crossed the line. She's willing to give up everything, but not that." David spoke steadily, incessantly. "She might be right. Perhaps this is the end of the road for us. We can't go on like this anymore."

"You need to give her time," I said, trying to draw closer to him. He turned on the faucet and began washing the dishes vigorously. He scrubbed the plates, bowls, and cutlery thoroughly, and rinsed them one by one. Once finished, he told me he was worn out and was going to lie down. He avoided my gaze and went upstairs. I heard him closing the door.

6

I woke up early the next morning. David was still asleep. I got out of bed and went downstairs. The lawyer hadn't responded to my last email. I answered a few emails. A friend from New York asked when I was coming to visit. There was an email from Dori, my brother, complaining that I'd disappeared and asking if I was okay. I answered as briefly as possible: *I'm on a business trip to the East, I'm swamped with work*, I wrote. I added that I was meeting with several suppliers and barely had time to catch my breath. *Let's be in touch when I get back*, I signed off. I sent the same wording, with slight changes, to everyone.

Then I opened a private browsing window. David was still asleep. I googled the names Tom, David, and Miriam with their last name, but I couldn't find anything. I googled various combinations of their names with the words *death*, *shooting*, *accident*, *couple*, *yard accident*, the name of the state, the name of the district. Finally, I found a brief news item. It was about David and Miriam's generous donation to establish a library in the pediatric department of a local hospital. The library was named after Tom. Above the news item was a small photo of David and Miriam standing on either side of a colorful bookcase. David wore sunglasses, his hair was thick and black. Miriam stood very straight, even then she was gray, and it wasn't just her hair, there was something ghostly about her.

David didn't leave the bedroom, and when I checked on him he said he wasn't feeling well. I went downstairs so he could rest, it was clearly something to do with Miriam. I tidied up the house and fixed breakfast. David came downstairs, he ate very little—he had no appetite—and after that he went straight back to bed. During the meal he made no effort, it felt as if he wasn't there. Sometime later, I went up to the bedroom to let him know I was going out to buy a few things. He appeared to be sleeping. His breaths were long and rhythmic.

On my way to the grocery store, I didn't think about David and Miriam very much. I was still anxious about my job. I kept on running different scenarios through my head. I saw in my mind's eye the CEO's utterly monstrous reaction to HR's announcement that I couldn't be fired because I was pregnant. A dead end.

When I returned a few hours later, David was not in the living room or the kitchen, and I presumed he was still resting upstairs in the bedroom. I didn't go up until I'd finished unpacking the groceries and had boiled water for tea. When I entered the bedroom, a cup of tea in hand, I saw the bed was neatly made. David's belongings were gone. I went downstairs and stood outside without a coat, but I came back in very quickly and closed the door. Only when I reentered the kitchen did I notice a piece of folded paper under the table. It must have fallen to the floor when I put the grocery bags on the table.

> *I had to go home*
> *You can stay here as long as you like*
> *I'll call tomorrow*
> *Take care of yourself*
>
> D

ALONE——

The thirteenth time I went shooting in America, I was alone. This was the first time I had ever gone hunting on my own. One thing was clear to me: If I concentrated hard enough, the bullet would hit whatever I wanted it to hit. It had been a long time since I had experienced blurriness and shaking, all that seemed to disappear when I began my mandatory vacation. I didn't think it would come back because whenever I went out hunting with David, whenever I aimed the rifle, I was able to focus on the target successfully.

The night before I went hunting alone, David called to ask how I was doing. Maybe he wanted to explain why he'd left like that, but I didn't give him a chance, nor did I ask him about his abrupt departure. I didn't even try figuring out how he got home without his truck. At the time I supposed things were still tense between him and Miriam, and I didn't want to get in their way. Perhaps Miriam knew about our relationship, I wasn't sure, but anyway it was none of my business, it was their problem. For me, it was more important to get information on where to hunt. David wasn't at home, he said he'd taken Miriam's car for a drive, to clear his head. I sat down in the kitchen with pen and paper to write down his instructions. It was the same sheet of paper David had used to write his note. I flipped it over. David told me where to go, where to start, when I should leave and come back. He told me which was the best trail. He spoke patiently, slowly, detailing place names, road numbers, pit stops for gas and food. He told me to keep an eye on the weather report the night before and again before setting out in the morning. "Sometimes the change in weather can be extreme," he said. The sheet of paper filled up, I interrupted him in the middle to go fetch more paper from my bag. "Since you're alone, it's essential to be alert to other hunters in the area. Out of every ten hunters, one or two won't follow the rules."

Before we'd finished going over everything, he broke off, said he would call again later, and hung up. I remained at the table, going over my notes. It all seemed straightforward, and yet I read his instructions over and over again.

My vigilance began first thing in the morning. I needed a different level of attention now. When I went out hunting with David, it was much easier. David drove and I sat next to him, it never bothered me where we were exactly or when we would get there. When we arrived at the grounds, I followed him. I stopped when he stopped, tensed up when he did, and shot when he told me to shoot.

I woke up early, fixed myself a bite to eat and a cup of coffee I didn't finish. Then I hit the road. The snow that fell all night had turned to ice, leaving the roads slippery. I drove slowly and kept my distance from trucks. When I reached the parking lot I recognized it immediately, I'd been here before with David. I got ready slowly, I removed the backpack and the rifle from the backseat. I wanted to be sure I didn't forget anything. I talked out loud to myself: "Here's the backpack, here's the rifle, the binoculars." I double-checked the map on my phone. I made sure I'd saved screenshots with varying degrees of close-ups so I would still have access to a map if I lost cell phone reception. Just to be on the safe side, I memorized the trail David had outlined and the landmarks he had pointed out. I switched the phone to silent and put it in the pocket of my storm suit. Although David didn't call me back as promised, I felt confident. I didn't have any more questions about venturing out on my own, I'd found most of the answers online, I got by on my own. The night before, while I waited for my dinner to heat up, I read through all the pages, all the instructions, and copied everything onto a clean page in neat handwriting. I tucked the folded page into my pocket, alongside my phone. In the morning I checked the forecast and hunting conditions online for any special up-dates. There were no new warnings, nothing that prevented me from driving out to the hunting grounds that morning.

I began walking. The backpack weighed me down, it was heavier than usual, but after a while I got used to it. I was focused on the trail.

Before leaving that morning, I checked my inbox again. The lawyer still hadn't responded to my last email about the pregnancy option. In about two weeks I'd know the verdict.

ılınılınıl

The air was freezing, and when I paused to wipe my nose, my fingers were numb. The rest of the time my face was covered with a woolen balaclava, with two holes for the eyes, like a burglar mask. I advanced slowly, it seemed I was the only one for miles. I couldn't hear anyone, there was no movement around me. The deeper I progressed into the wooded area, the easier it was to break free of the thoughts that troubled me about going back to work. Finally, after fifteen minutes of walking, I reached the first landmark, a tree with a metal sign nailed into its trunk:

To Dad
RIP
Your Loving Family

I kept going according to David's instructions. The snow was deep and crunched loudly under my feet. I progressed very slowly, and after another half hour of walking I reached the spot where David said I should take a break. And if I still had energy, he added, I could keep going. I decided to press on, and in another half hour I reached the second landmark. I glanced at my watch, it was only nine in the morning. From there it was supposed to be a quick walk to the planned resting place. This second landmark had been harder to identify, a low wooden fence that was covered in snow. I kicked a few chunks of icy snow to expose the fence and make it easier to recognize on my way back. I took a break. I removed the backpack, propped it up against the fence, and leaned against it. I took out some food, a sandwich and a banana. Everything was silent. I was alone. After eating the banana, I began walking again on the trail. I knew it was essential to be utterly focused here. I had a short distance to cover, and I would need to look for a place to set up. I made good progress and found a suitable place. I removed the backpack and placed it on the ground. I flattened the snow into a smooth surface and positioned myself comfortably on my elbows. I held the rifle securely between my hands and looked through the gunsight, I had a wide range of vision. I placed the rifle in the snow and scanned the area with my binoculars. I couldn't see anything. I took the rifle, loaded it with one bullet, and placed two more bullets on the snow. From time to time, I scanned the area with my binoculars. There was no movement.

I lay there for a while, motionless; I didn't look at my watch, I didn't want to move a muscle, so I had no idea how much time had passed. Just when I'd decided to call it a day and before I had time to get to my feet, I heard a rustling. I froze in place. The noise was so faint, I couldn't be sure. After a few moments, they appeared. One animal, and then another, about six hundred feet from me. They walked along, one following the other, and then paused. From where I lay, I couldn't tell what made them pause. I kept my gunsight trained on them.

The first shot hit the animal that stood to the right. A direct hit to the kill zone. I quickly reloaded the gun but failed to hit the other animal. It fled immediately, I watched it bounding away. I reloaded the rifle and fired a third shot at the animal stretched out on the ground, an unnecessary shot. My heart was pounding. I lay there in the snow for a few moments before retrieving the cartridges and getting to my feet. One, two, three cartridges. I put them in the pocket of my storm suit. The thought of Miriam crossed my mind briefly, the moment she discovered the cartridges in the backyard. Had those cartridges fallen out of my pocket?

I got up too quickly, became very dizzy, and almost lost my footing. I steadied myself and went back into a crouch. I waited a little and picked up the rifle from the ground. I grabbed the binoculars and focused them on the animal, there was something strange about it. I stood up again, this time more carefully. I hoisted the backpack over my shoulders and waited. I wanted to make sure it wasn't moving. Slowly, I advanced toward the animal and as I drew closer, I saw what had happened. Everything had gone horribly wrong.

I sprinted back to the car, running madly, holding the backpack and rifle. At one stage, I lost my footing in a snow drift and landed on the rifle with a sharp blow to my ribs. Right after the first blow came the second one as the backpack came crashing down on my head. Despite the pain, I scrambled to my feet and kept running. I located the fence, but it took me a while to find the tree. I went around in circles until I somehow found it. I came to a standstill in front of the sign nailed to the tree, I read it a few times, I wanted to be sure this was my tree, our tree. *To Dad RIP Your loving family*. I read it again and again until the words lost their meaning.

Back at the parking lot, I removed the phone from my pocket. My head and ribs still hurt. The reception was bad, but I dialed anyway. The call didn't go through, there was no way it could have gone through, there wasn't even a dial tone. I tossed the backpack into the truck with one swift movement and removed the rifle from my shoulder. I almost hit myself in the face with the rifle. Then I made sure it wasn't loaded. I aimed the rifle toward the sky and checked the chamber was clean. There was no real need to do this since it wasn't an automatic rifle and I'd already used all the bullets. It was an old habit that had resurfaced.

I was still alone. I laid the rifle in the back and circled the truck. I got inside and slammed the door. I locked myself in and looked through the windows and mirrors. There was no one there at all, I was completely alone. I revved up the engine and turned the heat on. My heart was beating fast. I tried to calm down, but I couldn't. I just couldn't. My heart was still pounding in my chest. I didn't want to start driving until I'd calmed down. I stared ahead at a pile of snow. I rummaged through David's truck. I was looking for something, anything at all. A protein bar, something to put in my mouth. I found cigarettes in the glove compartment. God knows how long they'd been lying there. I didn't know David smoked, or perhaps he'd quit. I took a cigarette and pressed the cigarette lighter. When it popped up, I took the lighter out of the socket and lit the cigarette. I opened the window and leaned over to open the window of the passenger seat too. I took several drags on the cigarette and wanted to throw up. I managed to open the door, but half my body was still inside the vehicle. I threw up everything I had eaten that day. I tossed the cigarette, immediately regretted it, and retrieved it. I covered everything with the freezing snow. The snow on my bare hands felt like needles piercing through my flesh to the bones, through my fingernails. I took a bottle of water from the backpack. I washed my face and rinsed my mouth with water. My face was freezing, but it didn't matter anymore, nothing mattered, I had to wake up from this nightmare. I got back into the truck and closed the windows. I drove back to the highway. My phone was useless, the reception was weak and there was hardly any battery left. I stopped off at the roadside diner where David and I had sat a few days earlier. I remembered there were public phones there, I inserted two quarters into the coin slot and dialed the number with numb fingers. I was shaking all over. One ring, two, three, eternity until I heard David's voice: "Hello."

David sounded tired and distant, not at all like himself. I told him we needed to meet back at the house. My tone was decisive. "I need you to come right now," I said. There was silence, as if it took him a moment to figure out who I was or why I was calling. I repeated my words, I said I had to see him, he had to come, and he asked, "Come where?" and I said, "Here, to the house, the one we stayed in together until yesterday, until you left." He responded with a grunt, and then a weird, forced cough. "I can't make it today, I'm sorry, I have some things to do at home this evening. Let's meet up some other time." There was a murmuring, perhaps it was Miriam's voice, I couldn't be sure, and after another pause, "Speak soon," he said, and hung up. It was only when I heard the line go dead that I realized he'd hung up on me. It was a terrible sound, a deafening one. My head was throbbing. I slammed the phone receiver down in its cradle and it fell, swinging from the cord, knocking against the wall. I could still hear the beeping of the disconnected line as I left the phone booth. It sounded like a hospital monitor, when the line on the screen straightens out, parallel to the floor. It was the first time David had spoken to me with such coldness. After that, things moved fast. I got into the car and drove back to the house. I don't remember the road that joined the two points. Inside, I went to the kitchen table, where I'd left my laptop, and switched it on. I opened a private browsing window, typed in *missing person*, and in another private window typed in the name of a local news site. The search didn't produce anything. I left the windows open with the searches and clicked refresh every few minutes. I opened another window and checked my inbox. There was an email waiting for me from my lawyer:

> Congratulations!
>
> Yes, we can work with this. Let's see how the pregnancy progresses, that everything's okay. Anyway, let's speak at the beginning of next week.

She signed off with holiday greetings, although I wasn't sure which holiday she was referring to, perhaps Hanukkah. I didn't respond to her email. I went out to the truck, grabbed the backpack and the rifle, and dashed back into the house. I didn't feel cold. I thrust my hand into my pocket and pulled out the cartridges. I counted them again, one, two, three.

I placed the cartridges on the kitchen table and counted them again. One, two, three. I kept refreshing the pages but there were no updates, nothing. There was nothing online at all.

———

The little appetite I had disappeared completely that evening. I ate nothing the next morning either. At night, in bed, I got no sleep. I tossed and turned from side to side. I kept hearing David's cold voice, but mostly what kept me from falling asleep was the sight of the dead animal bleeding into the snow and the body lying near it, face down in the snow, and what was clearly a hand, a human hand.

By morning, a decision had formed in my head. I had to go back to ascertain whether one of my bullets had hit the person lying there. I was pretty sure I had only hit the animal. I hoped so.

By seven o'clock I was already in the truck. The backpack was lighter this time. I packed only drinking water and a green apple. I took the rifle and put three bullets in my pocket, just in case. I wasn't planning on hunting. I just wanted to get there, do what I had to do and leave.

I was lucky it had not snowed the night before. The weather report predicted a storm that would last several days. My hunting trip was over. Soon, I was due back at work. There was no other option.

|ıııılıııl|

I didn't need to consult the map or memorize anything. I parked the truck and got out quickly. I grabbed the backpack and the rifle. I adjusted the straps of the backpack and hoisted it onto my back. I counted the three bullets in the pocket of my storm suit.

The sun shone with a faint, murky light. A wintry fog covered the entire area. I saw no one else that morning. I set out, walking quickly. I reached the tree easily and then the fence. I was on the right track. I felt my pulse quickening as I proceeded. While walking, I tried to take deep breaths to calm myself. I paused by the fence for a few moments and then continued walking. I reached the point where I had crouched down the day before. I raised the binoculars, scanned the area, and spotted the bodies lying there, exactly where I remembered the point of impact with the target. Before proceeding, I surveyed the area again with my binoculars. I wanted to be sure there was no one else around. The last thing I needed was for someone to see me there. I didn't trouble myself with the thought that someone might have seen me the day before. I went over to the exact spot; everything was different, this was not the scene that had haunted me all night. Both bodies were evidently frozen, the large animal and a smaller one beside it. I wasn't sure what I was looking at. They lay side by side, two animals, like a little family. The wind whipped up, and I moved toward the big animal that lay to the right. I located one shot in the kill zone. Then I moved on to the second animal. It was hard to see anything, the animal was in an advanced state of freezing, entirely covered in ice. I searched the smaller animal's body for an entry point. I examined every inch of its little body.

I found nothing. Perhaps I had imagined it, perhaps it didn't happen. Again, I counted one shot in the first animal, and surveyed the body of the little one, lying by its side. I removed the phone from my pocket and took photos of both animals from various angles. I studied the photos carefully, they also showed the two animals lying side by side. I stayed there for a few moments, then began walking back, but after twenty or thirty paces I stopped and retraced my steps. I wanted to check once more. This time I removed the balaclava from my face, I wanted to see everything as clearly as possible. The air was frozen, the two animals were lying in precisely the same position as they had a few minutes earlier.

It was early noon when I got back to David and Miriam's vacation home. Everything happened so fast, my heart was pounding and I had to do something. I went upstairs and changed the sheets. From there I continued to the bathroom, where I removed all the towels off the hooks: hand towels, bath towels. I tossed everything in a pile in the hallway. I scrubbed down the bathroom, the toilet too, I polished the floor, the ceramic tiles on the walls, I scrubbed the sink and the toilet bowl, the faucets, I got down on my knees and scrubbed the floor with my bare hands. On my way downstairs to the kitchen, I tripped over something and almost tumbled down the stairs. Then I scrubbed the kitchen floor, the countertop, the sink. I opened the fridge and had to stop myself from emptying the entire contents of the fridge and cleaning that too. I rummaged through the closets until I found an old vacuum cleaner. I vacuumed the living room, the carpet, the couches, and the floor. After I finished cleaning the house I went down to the basement. I did a load of wash with all the sheets and towels, and threw in my own clothes, the ones I was wearing. When I went back upstairs, I was naked. I stretched out on the couch and tried to figure out how to keep going. I lay there, staring at the ceiling, waiting for something to happen, anything. After a while, the phone beeped. It was on the kitchen table, where I'd left it to charge. After the first beep there was another one, and then two more, the phone just wouldn't stop beeping. Text messages from David. Two of them were sent in the morning while I was out, they arrived late, probably because there was no reception. In the first message he wrote: *What's up? Is everything okay with you?* In the second: *Do you still want me to come over?* In the third: *Please let me know you're okay,* and in the final message he just wrote: *Sorry.*

We can meet when I get back, no need for you to come, I replied before I had time to regret it. I fished David's pack of cigarettes out of my coat pocket, and smoked two in a row. Then I went upstairs and took a very hot shower.

I had to go out. I realized there were a few stormy days ahead of me when I would be stuck in the house. I had to see people. I checked the weather report, a storm was expected the next morning. It was forecast to intensify and last several days. I searched for the nearest restaurant and went out to David's truck.

A few people were sitting at the bar, I ordered a beer and a snack. I barely glanced at the menu. It made no difference to me, my stomach was completely messed up. I finished the first beer and ordered another. I took out a cigarette and the man behind the bar came up to me. He said there was an unofficial smoking area in the back. "You can smoke there," he said. I moved over to the smoking area, which stank of cigarettes. I sat down and waited for a guy who was sitting there to make eye contact with me. I gestured with my cigarette. He pulled out a lighter and lit my cigarette but then turned around to the girl sitting next to him, his back to me. They were talking loudly to each other, but I couldn't figure out what they were saying. I finished my second beer, I still didn't feel drunk, I needed more. More of something. I ordered bourbon on the rocks and took another cigarette, but when I turned to the guy with the lighter, he had disappeared. After a few minutes he came back, this time alone. I asked for another light, and he lit it.

"You're not from here, are you?"

The restrooms were empty and smelled bad. I glanced at myself in the mirror. There were deep, dark circles under my eyes, and wrinkles at the edges. The wrinkles were deeper and more pronounced than the last time I looked. I entered one of the stalls, and as I locked it behind me, I heard the door creak, a few steps, a knock, and then another one.

We did it standing up. I leaned forward onto the filthy wall and he entered me. I wanted to come but I also wanted to be over and done with it as quickly as possible and to leave. I wanted to go back to the house and sleep for an entire day, perhaps two days. He panted, picking up momentum. "Is it good for you?" he groaned. I yelled at him to shut up, which turned him on even more. He kept pounding away until I came. I pushed him away immediately. I gave him a hand job and he ejaculated over the toilet bowl. He closed the lid of the toilet and sat down on it, wasted. I left him there and went through the bar and out to the parking lot. When I got to the truck, I realized I'd forgotten my parka. A shot of bourbon awaited me at the bar when I went back inside. I took a sip, grabbed my parka, and left the bar. My head was buzzing from all the alcohol, and as I reversed out of the parking lot, the truck skidded on the ice and I almost hit a car.

On the way back, I switched on the radio, turning it up louder and louder, yelling at myself over the noise of the radio, hoping not to pass out. I opened the window a crack and a blast of bitterly cold air entered, hitting me in the face.

———

In the days that followed I was angry with David, an anger that only intensified. I hoped to let that anger go before I returned home. Or at least before I returned to work. I still wasn't sure where things stood. In any case, David was not just my only friend at work, he was my only friend. I hadn't made an effort to meet people since I'd arrived. I had a few last days remaining until the end of my vacation and a few days remaining until my period arrived, if at all. Who knows, David might be the father of my only child. Thanks to David, I might be able to put plan B into action: the pregnancy that would save me from returning to Israel, the baby who would keep me at work.

The weather report predicted large amounts of snow over the area. This calmed me down, the thought that winter would end and they would eventually be found, side by side. It would be impossible to reconstruct the specific hour or even day. My tracks would have completely disappeared. And in any case, my bullets did not hit the frozen animal. I replayed it over and over in my head, what I saw when I went back the second time. Everything was a mess, the terrible scene manifested itself once more before my eyes. I shook myself. "Those were two animals," I said loudly, almost shouting.

On the morning of my last day in David and Miriam's vacation home I wrote briefly to my lawyer, saying I was going back to work, that we'd catch up. That all options were open.

When my mom called that morning, I didn't pick up. Later I wrote her that I had meetings all day and couldn't talk. I asked if everything was okay. She wrote me back that all was well, that she was just calling to see how I was. *Yes, all good, just a little busy, don't worry*, I replied.

When I finally arrived home, after a long and exhausting journey, the house was freezing. It was my fault this time, I had turned down the heat to the bare minimum before going out. I didn't want to leave it on while I was away. The house was too cold to stay in, so I turned up the heat and drove to the only restaurant still open in the area. Just before I left, I texted David, inviting him to join me. I said he could take his car back at the same time. David didn't respond, but shortly after sitting down I saw him enter the restaurant. He scanned the tables, searching for me. When he spotted me, he paused for a moment before coming over. I said nothing as he sat down opposite me, just gently pushed my glass of bourbon toward him.

"I don't know how to apologize for that evening, and the next day, and the afternoon when you asked me to come and I hung up without explaining anything," he said, his words flooding out.

"First, I'm going to use the restroom. While I'm gone, order us something to eat. Order meat, I feel like eating meat."

———

I patted his hand, almost stroked it, and his hand trembled for a moment. On the way to the restroom, I thought I saw Joan's image reflected in the mirror that lined the walls of the restaurant. Her face seemed puffier, her hair was a little longer, and sitting with her was a man, probably her husband. It had been a while since I last saw her, maybe four months. When I passed her table, I realized it wasn't Joan, she only slightly resembled her, a tall woman whose face was rounder than Joan's and whose hands were clasped over her pregnant belly.

As soon as I pulled down my underwear in the restroom, I knew it. My period had arrived all at once. I sat down on the toilet seat, I couldn't have cared less how filthy it was, I wiped my underwear as best I could, rolled up a piece of toilet paper and soaked up the rest of the blood. Then I used a fresh roll of toilet paper to line my underwear. I stood in front of the mirror and washed my hands thoroughly, I looked gray. Just before I walked back to the table, I noticed a basket of tampons by the sink. I took the fattest tampon there was and went back into the stall. When I washed my hands for the second time, someone came into the restroom, she smiled at me, and I smiled back. On my way to the table, I felt a wave of gloom creeping up on me. The waiter came, he placed wineglasses on the table and presented the bottle first to me and then to David. David nodded his head and signaled the waiter to pour me wine first. All this was good timing for me. It gave me an extra moment to come to terms with the situation. I picked up the wineglass and held it to my nose, I inhaled deeply. Then I swished the wine around the glass in a circular motion and brought it up to my nose to inhale the aroma again. I took a sip and said the wine was good. My voice shook. The waiter poured David a glass of wine, placed the bottle on the table, and left. As we clinked glasses, I said "Cheers" and my voice was so faint I could barely hear myself. The waiter returned with two small plates. He placed bread and butter on the table between us. I didn't wait for David. I was ravenous. I cut myself a slice of bread, I spread butter on it. I did this again and again. The waiter returned with the main courses and after that he placed a huge Caesar salad in the middle of the table. I started laughing, an evil kind of laugh, one that came from the bottom of the barrel, from the deep. David cut a juicy piece of steak and put it in his mouth.

"You know, I was hoping to get pregnant."

David stopped chewing and swallowed the piece of steak all at once, I watched it go down his throat until it came to a halt above his Adam's apple.

"But don't worry, my womb's more like a tomb."

David went quiet.

"It's such a small difference, just one letter, but there you go, I've got a tomb down there."

He stared at me.

"In Hebrew, the word 'tomb,' *kever*, is just one letter away from the word 'man,' *gever*."

Then I went quiet too.

I chewed my food, I chewed all the food on my plate. Meanwhile the waiter placed another basket of bread and butter on the table.

At the end of the meal I asked the waiter if I could get the salad to go, although I knew I wasn't going to eat it, especially after a day or two in the fridge.

We walked out of the restaurant to the closed terrace—an area that was not as warm as the restaurant but not as freezing as outside. When I gave David the keys to the truck, he gripped my hand. I didn't resist when he pulled me close, and we stood like this for a few more moments until he loosened his hold. He drove me home. When he stopped at the entrance to my house, I got out immediately. I slammed the door and walked off, I didn't look back to see if he was still there, if he was checking I'd entered the house safely and that I'd closed the door behind me.

|ılılıılıılıılıılıl

The day I returned from vacation I arrived at the office earlier than usual. The first meeting on my calendar, with Dan, had been planned weeks in advance. My plan was to carry on as normal, I was back from vacation, that was all. This was what my lawyer advised me to do as well. David called me on the office phone line, which was strange since he usually sent a text message or came to my office when he wanted something. He asked me to come to the conference room near the cafeteria, he said he needed me for something. I told him I had a meeting with the CEO and asked if it was urgent. He said it would be brief, no more than ten minutes. There were very few people at work, I couldn't see anyone in the cafeteria. It seemed like winter was slowing everything down.

When I entered the conference room, David was waiting for me. Before I even sat down, he said the CEO would not be coming. The office in Israel had asked him to handle this.

"They've changed their minds and offered me a new five-year contract," he began, his face composed. I did not react, and he continued. He said that in the three weeks of our absence complete chaos had ensued.

"Two big clients threatened to drop us, that's why Dan isn't coming, he and the VPs are working on damage control."

He went on talking, detailing priorities, schedules, and critical tasks. By this stage I wasn't listening, I just stared at him and watched his mouth as it moved. But I still didn't understand what was happening, what was happening to me, what was happening in general. When he paused, I asked about my position, whether they'd updated him about that.

"They kept insisting there was no need for your position, but I stood my ground."

The room began spinning. First the table, then David, then the door.

"Are you okay?" His hand patted mine.

"Yes, I think I'm a little dehydrated, that's all."

I poured myself a glass of water, and David got to his feet.

"Anyway, as I said, in the end you'll be working with me, you're transferring to the American team. It's a done deal, you can say goodbye to Israel." He laughed.

I didn't quite get what he meant. I didn't quite get the procedure. Was I supposed to quit, or were they supposed to fire me? And then what would happen, would the company in the US hire me?

David looked at me and said, "You see, I told you there was nothing to worry about." He held out both hands. I didn't even flinch, and after a moment he folded his hands across his chest in embarrassment.

"We fixed it," he said.

David looked happier than he'd looked in a long while. I wasn't sure if this was a good thing, or if it was bad. I lost my sense of place, of time. I didn't know what to say. I wanted to get out of there, to go back to my office, to my computer, to go through the emails that had piled up since that meeting with the CEO, to start everything all over again. Before the vacation, before the meeting with the CEO, further and further back, before I got to the US, before I landed. Before everything.

LEAVING ——

1

had decided right away to accept the relocation
offer. Nevertheless, I waited. I wanted to let the idea
percolate for a while, I didn't want them to think I was jumping
at the offer. But as soon as Tal opened his mouth and said they
had a job offer for me, as soon as he said the word *abroad*—I
knew. It was clear to me the opportunity had arrived. I saw the
point of exit, the open door, I saw them holding that door wide-
open for me. All I had to do was decide when I wanted to step
over the threshold.

I kept a poker face while Tal was talking, I kept my cards
close to my chest. He droned on and on, I remained composed,
nodding my head now and again.

When I went back to my apartment that evening, I did a
dance in the living room. I'd never danced like that before, not
alone, not in front of the mirror, definitely not in the presence of
other people, I'd always been dance recalcitrant. I had nothing

against music itself, but my body always remained rooted to the spot, reluctant to join in. In the apartment block that faced mine, I watched a neighbor hanging up his laundry. Summer refused to let up, it was hotter than ever, hot as hell, like every summer, just a little worse.

The neighbor stood there, bare-chested, pinning undershirts and boxer shorts, all of them white. I didn't know him by name. From time to time, I heard the dull sound of pins landing on the awning of the apartment below. Between hanging up undershirts he raised his eyes and stared at me through my open window, and when I stared back he didn't look away. I kept on dancing even though he was watching; I knew that soon enough I'd never see him again, I couldn't have cared less. He finished hanging up the laundry and went inside. I watched him dragging the shutters along the metal track and then opening them. He continued spying on me through the open shutters. I saw his silhouette, hunched over.

That evening, I couldn't decide who to call first with the news that I was leaving for the US. In the end I picked Dori, but he was on a call, so I hung up. I tried him again, and he sent me a text message that he was in the middle of something, that we'd speak tomorrow, but if it was urgent I should text him.

2

I broke the news a few days later, at our regular Friday night family dinner. I told them all together, Dori, Mom, and Dad. I'd prepared a detailed statement of defense.

"It's an excellent opportunity to earn the money to buy an apartment." I began with the final line, the most persuasive one. I spoke decisively, I quoted huge sums of money, I may have exaggerated my salary a little. I told them about the relocation package and the expense account they'd opened for me. "And naturally they'll cover my housing costs," I added for good measure. Dad nodded, he chewed a piece of bread dipped in tahini and another spicy condiment, left on the table at the end of the meal. Dori listened, slurping his tea noisily. Only Mom stared at me in shock, her eyes shining, she looked like she'd stopped breathing, someone whose breath had caught for a moment, and then forever. Dad swallowed another morsel of bread and then interrupted—good, good, excellent, excellent, good, good—as he always did in moments of tension. Repeating the same word twice was like pressing the rewind button, a reset of some sort. Dori asked where I was moving, to which city, how I would get there, through which airport, technical questions that somewhat eased the general atmosphere. Mom stuck to her silence and didn't say a word, and from the expression on her face it was clear to me that she got the picture right away. That this was final, a done deal, and I would be alone, forever. Gone was the chance to see me with a husband, and daydreaming of grandchildren was out of the question. She'd always been afraid to speak to me about this, but she didn't have to say anything. It was clear how she felt about the choices I had made in life.

3

On my final Rosh Hashanah in Israel, my mom invited the entire family over for a festive meal. No one knew my plan was to never come back. "She's going for a couple of years, maybe less, and then she'll be back, a temporary assignment," Mom said to one of her cousins. I helped her serve generous amounts of food to the guests that evening. I'd arrived early that morning to set the table, clean up a bit, and help with last-minute chores. We were twenty adults and a few of my cousins' kids around that table. "So, what are you up to these days?" I was asked, although no one asked if I was in a relationship; perhaps Mom had cautioned them to steer clear of forbidden topics: a boyfriend, children. The jokes were the same jokes from last year. My cousin's husband, a dentist, told the same joke he'd been telling for the past fifteen years, maybe even longer. The joke was at my expense, but the main character was his friend's daughter. "She completed a degree in electrical engineering, four years of bloodletting. She graduated with honors! From the Technion Institute of Technology!" he began.

It went without saying that on her first day at work she decided to quit. He claimed she didn't know this profession would be so physical. "She found herself in a factory!" He laughed wholeheartedly, exposing unnaturally white teeth. I first heard this joke when I was still in university. I went to him for a checkup, and he cracked the joke as I lay there, my mouth wide-open under the lights, a drill in his hand. I promised myself never to go back to him for treatment.

As well as helping my mom that morning, I also used the time to empty the closet in my childhood bedroom. Like Dori's bedroom, mine had also become a storeroom for my parents' belongings. But the closet was also full of my own things. I threw everything into the trash. All the notepads and college textbooks that had ended up there. All the paychecks I'd ever received, meticulously arranged in plastic sleeves, filed away in binders according to year and place of employment. My childhood bedroom had become my own private archive. Why on earth had I kept all this paperwork? I got rid of it all. Trash bag after trash bag filled to bursting. Letters, birthday cards, photos from trips abroad, watches, sheet music, old clothes, study guides for college entrance exams, frayed army fatigues, photos of people I barely remembered. At the back of the shoe drawer, I found an empty cartridge from an M16 rifle. I threw that in the trash too.

4

I emptied my apartment and packed up my belongings in a single day. All that remained were two crates filled with books. I gave away some of the pictures that had hung in my apartment and left the rest outside my building for someone to take. I took a break around noon and went to get a falafel on the outskirts of the neighborhood. It was just me and a bunch of men from the nearby stores and car shops. We stood at the long, aluminum counter, eating with half-open mouths, dribbling drops of tahini and spicy amba sauce onto the counter. When I finished eating, I noticed my shirt was stained with amba, but it made no difference, I threw it in the trash as soon as I got back to the apartment. I went back to emptying out my closet. Two suitcases stood in the center of the living room, although there was a week to go before my departure. I knew it would be much colder than Israeli winters, with below-zero temperatures. I spent time going through my winter clothing, I sorted all the socks, and I packed almost all the underwear. Moments after packing the underwear and socks I changed my mind and removed the underwear from the suitcase. I inspected them again, threw most in the trash, and kept just a few. I decided to either buy a few more pairs at one of the airports where I had a connecting flight or simply wait until I arrived. I went through the rest of the clothes, and anything that didn't look good, or didn't fit, went straight into the trash. Eventually, one suitcase was full and the other was almost empty. Lined up against the wall were trash bags filled with most of my clothes. When I saw all the bags lined up like that, I almost regretted my decision. I considered starting all over again, perhaps I'd missed something that I actually liked. But the phone rang, interrupting my train of thought. It was his name that appeared on the screen.

He was calling after two years of silence. I debated whether to answer or not, I was sure I'd deleted his name from my contacts. The phone rang a few times and then stopped. He must have hung up.

5

Less than a week before my departure, Mom and I met for coffee. She suggested a café I'd never been to before. On any other occasion I would have insisted we meet somewhere a little nicer. But I didn't care anymore, I was already feeling that tingling sensation in the soles of my feet, that feeling of airiness under the rug, I was imagining the moment when I would be able to see the clouds through the airplane window. The minute she sat down, she began nagging me with her usual barrage of questions. What did I pack, did I make an appointment to see the dentist, the family doctor, the gynecologist, had I put together a first aid kit for myself, had I finished taking care of the car, did I cancel the insurance. Finally, she asked if I'd spoken to him. As usual, she refrained from calling him by name, as though he were some state secret. When she said "to him" she stressed the second word as though that might actually be his name, Him. She slipped in that last question about Eran at the end of a long list of general questions, as if it were one of the tasks I had to complete before my departure, before leaving. I answered all her questions quickly, dryly, *yes, no, tomorrow, it's on my list,* but I hesitated before answering her last question. "I didn't talk to Eran, there's no point." She scowled. My mom knew about the pregnancy, but she never managed to figure out what was going on between us, and what happened in the end. In fact, she hoped it wasn't over, Eran seemed to her like my last chance, her last chance. "He's single, so what's the problem, I don't understand," she used to say. When we were together, she would ask about him offhandedly, briefly, because she knew she was playing with fire. I always knew there were other questions she wanted to ask, more urgent ones hovering on the tip of her tongue, questions she kept from slipping out of her mouth and into the empty space, the vacuum she regarded as my life. She couldn't understand why we didn't live together, and why he never joined our family dinners. She knew about the abortion. But she didn't know all the details. I also knew she herself had miscarried between Dori and me.

A day or two after my abortion, when I was feeling better and she came to visit, I told her I was relieved in a way, that I wasn't sure I was ready for it. She hugged me and said, "Don't worry, there'll be others."

————

After breakfast we went to the museum. Since retiring, she'd gotten into the habit of going to an exhibition once a month or so. A new photography exhibit had just opened, and a friend suggested they go together, but she preferred to go with me. "I won't have that many more opportunities," she added.

"Of course you will," I said adamantly, and changed the subject. I asked her numerous questions, about the friend she was taking a course in modern Judaism with, about the course she'd signed up for in Hebrew literature at the Central Library, about the excursions she was planning.

I exhausted her with my questions, and she begged me to stop cross-examining her. "What's up with you today?" she finally asked.

When I got home, I got a message from Eran, he'd be waiting for me at a local bar that evening. I still hadn't decided whether to see him or not. I had almost no clothes left in the closet and wasn't about to stress over what I should wear. The suitcase was packed. The apartment was empty, aside from the bed, the wall-mounted bookcase in the living room, the two suitcases, and a few items of clothing in the closet I'd planned to get rid of. I lay on the bed listlessly.

I woke up when the phone rang. It was Eran, he was already there.

6

It came out of the blue. He said he wanted to try again. That he got it now, that everything was clear to him, he'd gotten his priorities straight, his work, and everything else. When he said that, I laughed, seriously!

"Really, I laughed out loud. It took me a few seconds to regain myself but when I stopped laughing and looked at him again, he repeated his words, and it seemed as if he meant it.

"I didn't know what to say. I kept quiet, and then I reminded him that two years had gone by, two years!

"That was the only thing that went through my head, that two years had gone by.

"We sat there drinking. We chitchatted, about the city, about the insanity of e-bikes that had taken over the streets, unrelated stuff. By the way, he told me something crazy, a colleague of his from the office got run over by a guy on an e-bike. He was getting off the bus and hadn't taken two steps on the sidewalk. He ended up with two broken ribs and a concussion.

"We drank some more and I started feeling lightheaded and told him I'd eaten nothing since breakfast. We got a large pizza, and went back to my place, there were a few beers in the fridge. I told him the apartment was empty because I was renting it out for a month, maybe longer, that I was traveling for work. Basically, I lied.

"We sat on the floor of the balcony and he started again, said he felt he'd wasted all that time, he begged for another chance, he couldn't wrap his brain around the way we'd missed out on that pregnancy. It freaked me out that he said *we*, that we both missed out. I was so mad at him, I stopped feeling anything at all.

"After what he said, I reminded him I was going away for a month, maybe longer, that I didn't want to bring it all up again. That it wasn't the right time. I repeated it had been two years, and that it was unbelievable, him coming here like this out of nowhere. That was the only way of shutting him up, and he dropped the subject for the rest of the evening. He asked me how work was, idle chatter. At a certain stage I got fed up with all this beating around the bush, so I said: 'Do you want to fuck or was there something else you had in mind?'

"I went straight into the bedroom and stripped. A few moments later he was already groaning above me like an animal, he came quickly, as always, before I was even halfway there. Afterward he just lay there, exhausted.

"And then I told him to go, I didn't want him to stay the night."

The entire time I was telling her how things unfolded, barely missing a detail, Anat listened without saying a word.

"We failed the Bechdel Test," she said when I finished telling her. "You've talked only about him, for the last half hour, a guy who's a piece of garbage, the person who hurt you the most, he's the absolute worst." She couldn't figure out why I even answered the phone when he called.

"You're moving away, let's talk about that. He belongs to the past, it's dead and gone."

We strolled to the end of the promenade, it was a balmy evening with a pleasant sea breeze. I was happy to be going away, I wanted to leave everything and everybody behind. I would finally have some peace and quiet, I thought. It was exactly what I needed, at least for now. She nodded, as if she understood, as if she could read my thoughts. At that precise moment, I left her behind too.

That was the day I knew with certainty that I would never come back, that I would do anything not to come back, either to Eran or anyone else.

After we said goodbye at the square, I stood there watching her climb the stairs. Even from behind it was clear that her big belly weighed her down, she pushed herself up the steps, her left hand supporting her lower back, her right hand gripping the stone handrail. When she stopped for a moment, perhaps to catch her breath, I turned around and sat on the steps as if to tighten the knot of one of my shoelaces. When I stood up and turned, she was no longer there. Instead of walking back down the promenade to the south, I continued north. After a while I began running toward the other end of the promenade, then I ran through the park, stopping a couple of times to drink from the water fountains. I ran a lap around the park, went back to the promenade, and from there continued southward, picking up the pace as I ran.

7

The farewell party took place the Thursday be- fore my departure. Most of my department showed up, only the engineers who were meeting clients in Central Amer- ica were absent. Both the VP of engineering and the VP of busi- ness development came. There were cakes, which explained the large turnout. The espresso machine, hot water dispenser, and a few cartons of milk had been moved to the conference room. I didn't want speeches or gifts, and Tal promised not to make a big deal out of it. "It's not like I'm retiring," I said.

All at once, everyone started clapping, I'm not sure who began it. Uri, whose cubicle was next to mine, yelled out, "Speech, speech!" and a few others joined in—and then everyone looked at me, waiting for me to say something.

"Here's to everyone's health and happiness," I said, raising a slice of cake on a disposable plate. All eyes were fixed on me.

"It's been a blast working with you all, and now let's enjoy ourselves and I'll speak to you from the other side," I ended with a smile.

That was my last day in the office. I'd already taken most of my belongings or distributed them among colleagues. There were a few more bureaucratic details to iron out with Human Resources. I sat facing my computer, waiting for my meeting with them, browsing news sites, checking my inbox. For a moment I regretted my decision. Perhaps I'd made a mistake with Eran, perhaps there was another way.

On Monday morning, three days before my departure, I received two text messages from him. He'd sent them the night before but I only saw them in the morning, just before I left for the gynecologist.

When are you coming back?
I get the feeling I'm never going to hear from you again.

These messages eliminated the possibility that had opened. I felt surer than ever that the move was final, that I wouldn't return. My appointment was a follow-up, after completing a series of tests the gynecologist had asked me to do—blood work, an ultrasound, and another test I had to do in a private lab. She went over the results on her computer, murmured a few things to herself, and told me that I was still in good shape, very good shape, in fact. And then she turned serious and said that this was no indication of the future, that no one could promise me this would still be the case in a month, or two months. Taking into account my age and my "past surgical history," she recommended egg retrieval and freezing, it would save a lot of heartache, effort, and money later. "You don't want to wake up too late for the party," she said. During these moments she appeared like an extension of my mom. I saw in her eyes that same spark. I told her I would schedule an appointment for further consultations. I said nothing about going away.

While she printed out the after-visit summary and further referrals, she suggested I make haste. "I'm talking about a donation, of course, a sperm donation."

She didn't ask if there was a significant other in my life. I thanked her, I said I was thinking about it, that I would keep thinking about it.

When I left the clinic, I removed the summary and referrals from my bag and, without differentiating between them, bunched them together, ripped them in half, and then ripped them again. I dumped them in the first trash can I came across.

That was the end point. I was done with all the medical obligations on my list: teeth, ovaries, breasts. I picked up my winter jacket from the dry cleaner. I bought all the medication on my mom's list. I still hadn't decided whether to answer those text messages and, if so, what to write.

8

On Monday, two days before my departure, I woke up very early. The apartment was empty, the two suitcases stood in the living room, waiting. Morning light slipped through the shutters, and the apartment was exposed in all its ugliness. The empty walls, the windows that had gathered dust, the floor, devoid of rugs or furniture. I tried closing my eyes and going back to sleep, but I couldn't.

I browsed through the photo gallery on my phone and began scrolling backward. I wanted to find pictures of the apartment from better days, photos of the plants, the furniture, the airy living room, proof of the life it once held. I found several photos, really lovely ones. In one photo, I even spotted Eran. We were in the bedroom, I was on the bed, my face to the mirror, smiling. Eran was sitting on the desk, his back to the mirror. I clicked on the photo, I wanted to delete it, but I changed my mind and pressed cancel instead.

9

The evening before my departure I watched the late-night news on my laptop. I wasn't used to doing this, watching the news, as if I'd been preparing to disconnect for years. I'd let go of the need to know what was happening. I didn't want to know anything. The news anchor spoke with pathos, and I couldn't be sure if this was a newscast or some kind of entertainment show.

Afterward, I sat on the couch and stared at the stain on the empty wall where the TV screen had been. I had no plans for my last evening, I didn't have the strength to say goodbye to anybody, I had no wish to turn anyone into the last person I met on my last evening in the city.

Earlier that evening I took a walk down a nearby boulevard. Two girls were walking ahead of me, one of them was talking in a loud voice: "You see, there's no one to vote for, I'm dying to vote for the right, but they're all religious fanatics."

When I reached home, I wrote him a text message: *I'll be in touch when I get back*, but I erased it right away.

The evening before, when I said goodbye to my parents, my mom cried, my dad hugged her and then he drew me close and hugged me too, and the three of us stood like that. Dori showed up late after work and drove me back to Tel Aviv. When I got out of the car, and just before I shut the door, he said: "Bye, sis."

The evening before my departure, fatigued by the news, I watched a TV series on my laptop, a Scandinavian thriller. Suddenly there was an explosion, I was positive it came from the laptop. Five minutes later my mom called to tell me a missile had fallen in central Israel. I said this was Hamas saying goodbye to me, and I laughed. My mom didn't think it was funny. Then she said it was unclear who was responsible for launching the missile. In the background I could hear the TV, they were watching the news at full volume.

At noon I checked in for my flight, then I emailed David my flight details. I noticed he'd updated his profile picture. I enlarged it, I was sure we'd met before, maybe at one of the company events hosted in Israel. For my last dinner I ordered sushi and a noodle salad. When I finished eating, I went to throw the trash out, but the trash can under the building was overflowing. I walked down the street to the next trash can, and the next one, I almost reached the end of the street. I left the bag by the last can and went back to my apartment.

I took the last remaining beer out of the fridge and went out to the balcony. I could hear the neighbors fucking, their window was open, I'd never heard them fucking before. Sometimes they moaned in unison, sometimes only one of them moaned. I stayed out there, but at some point I stopped listening. I'd already left. I was still there in body, but that was all.

That night, before falling asleep, I tapped out a message to Eran:

You're probably right

It was still quite early, but I was exhausted and fell asleep immediately.

10

It was a short drive to the airport. The highway from Tel Aviv was empty, aside from a few taxis and trucks. The taxi driver was engrossed the entire way in conversation with his son, his voice charred by cigarettes. His son was speaking from some army base, but I heard only the driver's side of the conversation, because he was using earphones. The taxi driver encouraged him to stay on the base. "I know, *ya ibni*," he told him, "I went through hell, absolute hell, during my service, and later in reserve duty, but see here, one day all this will be over, it's not worth it, not worth it, you only have one more year left, *kharam*, such a shame, why get yourself thrown in jail? I'll see you next Saturday, call me whenever you're on night duty, I'll get you through it, I'm stuck in the taxi anyway, it's all the same to me. No, of course not, you're not bugging me. What about Moriah?"

And then he said, "Marina, sorry, Marina," and asked again,

"What about Marina?" and then he said, "Great, that's great" a few times, and then, "Invite her over on Saturday, she's a doll." Finally, he said, "Look after yourself, *ya ibni*," and hung up.

He pulled up to the curb, and I got out and went over to the line of baggage carts. I tried to take one, but it was locked. The driver yelled at me, "You need to swipe your credit card." After I released the cart he helped me stack the two suitcases. "Have a nice trip," he said and got back in the taxi and drove away.

Before entering the terminal building, I lingered outside for a moment. I inhaled the night air, the close and sweaty summer air, everything was humid and vaguely fetid. As always, the Israeli summer smelled like a carcass. I pushed the cart into the terminal, my flight was on the departure board. I checked my suitcases, the company had paid up front for the extra one. I breezed through security and passport control, from there I went through to the Duty Free area, I wandered around the stores a bit, but I didn't buy anything. I spent the time remaining before my flight at a table in the plaza by the fountain, I got myself some coffee and a bottle of water. For a moment I entertained the thought that something might happen on the flight and the plane would crash. That would have been a dumb way to die.

THE LAST SHOT ——

1

The fourteenth time I went shooting in America, it was springtime. They picked me up last and I sat with Sean in the back. Miriam sat up front in the passenger seat.

When David invited me to go out hunting that weekend, he didn't mention that Miriam and Sean would be joining us. Not that it would have made a difference if he'd told me, I would have come anyway.

My first year in America was coming to an end. Transferring over to the American team had brought with it relief. Daily communication with the directors in Israel gradually fizzled out, I preferred it that way. I was on the American side, a regional employee, not working for HQ. I owed nothing to anyone in Israel.

———

We walked to the first point on the trail. I was last, I followed with slow steps behind Sean. Eyes to the ground and forward, like swimming. I tried to concentrate, but I was distracted. After a while I let them get ahead, I had to pee. Sean kept going, and I kept my eyes on his back until he was out of sight. I got off the path and put my rifle down on the ground. When I was done, I went back to the path, picked up my rifle, and looked through the gunsight to see where they had turned. After scanning and rescanning the area I located them, flickering through the trees. I clearly recognized David and Sean, I couldn't find Miriam. I looked for her through the gunsight, I moved the rifle to the right and to the left, I couldn't see her.

Winter had left its mark, vegetation was sparse, but here and there were the first signs of blossoming, something worth waiting for. The early morning hours were chilly, but in the time that had passed since we got to the area, the sun had come out and the weather was nice, despite a cold wind. Miriam was with them. I caught up and we kept going. Miriam turned around to look at me a few times, perhaps she had noticed my disappearance, perhaps out of habit she checked again and again that no one was missing. Every time she turned around, she smiled at me. I smiled back.

During that first year I learned to smile properly. It wasn't that I didn't know how to smile before that, but the smile I'd acquired in Israel had something gloomy about it, something incomplete. "You've got a sad smile," said the man who took my passport photo before I left Israel. The new smile was complete, it revealed teeth but not gums, a corporate smile.

David stopped and we froze in place. He signaled us to get down, and we all obeyed. We waited for another signal and shifted from crouching to lying flat on the ground. At first I didn't see anything, all was quiet, no one moved. A few moments passed until I spotted it approaching, moving slowly through the trees, drawing closer. I tracked it through the gunsight of the rifle, the crosshairs were fixed precisely on the safe zone. The animal walked along peacefully, I didn't take my eyes off it, the crosshairs were fixed, I had a direct line of fire to the animal. Long moments passed, enough time to squeeze the trigger, load another bullet, aim the rifle, and fire again.

But I didn't. My eyes flickered uncontrollably. I blinked a few times but I had completely lost focus. Finally, the picture sharpened up. Boom, boom, I told myself. "Fire, fire," I said out loud. In the blur outside the gunsight's range of vision, I sensed a movement from one of the others. I didn't squeeze the trigger, the safety catch was on. I didn't shoot. My finger rested on the trigger guard, outstretched, pressing down hard on the metal. When I opened my other eye, everything that had been out of range returned to focus, and I saw David looking at me. He seemed a little annoyed, perhaps he was looking at Miriam, who lay between us, her eye trained on the crosshairs of her own rifle. I stared with one eye, beyond him, beyond the animal. Everything blurred and I couldn't see a thing. David turned his head back to his own rifle and exhaled. I was familiar with this gesture of his, the slow release of air from his lungs, a thin whistle that faded out. There was silence all around, I didn't shoot. The animal ambled along, and when the whistling faded there was a single shot. David missed the animal, and it bolted, it ran away. Deep inside, I gloated. I raised my eyes from the gunsight and the flickering disappeared. The scenery around me came back into focus. Sean surveyed the area with binoculars. His rifle lay beside him. I secured my rifle and pulled the charging handle to release the bullet from the chamber, but no bullet released. I was almost positive I had loaded the rifle.

David and Sean walked over to where the animal had paused, to check for signs of blood. David thought he might have hit it after all. I stayed behind and did not join them. Miriam and I waited for them to come back. We stood there in silence until Miriam asked if I was going back to Israel in the summer.

"You haven't been back for a year, you probably miss your friends, your family," she said.

"No," I replied, without giving it much thought. "I don't think I'll be going back this year."

Then she asked what the situation was out there, if it was still tense. "The situation is always tense," I told her laconically.

We walked back to the truck in the same order, first David, then Miriam, Sean, and me. At times we walked at exactly the same pace, like a platoon of soldiers. No one had heard a second shot and I wasn't even sure I'd fired it. I'd lost my direct line of fire to the animal, perhaps the bullet hit a tree trunk. There were no signs of blood in the area. No one hit anything.

Miriam talked to Sean all the way home, leaning toward him from where she sat up front. The sun shone down on the contours of her face, her straight gray hair. She looked more fragile than usual. Miriam asked Sean about his daughters, I didn't pay attention either to her questions or his answers.

When David stopped by the path leading up to my house I was surprised, I hadn't noticed the ride was over. Before he got out of the truck to help me with my things, he said they intended to go out hunting every week until the end of the season. "Yes, definitely, I'd be happy to join you," I heard Sean responding. "Yes, definitely, I'd be happy to join you too," I said. But my voice sounded muffled and distant, and only then did I realize I'd forgotten to remove my earplugs.

When I went around the back of the truck to get my things, David was already there, taking them out. Without my earplugs the noise level was unbearable, the closing of the door, the slamming of the trunk, everything was amplified.

That same evening, I spoke to my parents. They told me they were planning a summer vacation in Greece. When they asked how I was doing, if I knew what my schedule was, if I could take some time off, I avoided answering. I said something about a big project I was going to have to work on through the summer. In the middle of the conversation my mom said something, and her voice sounded amplified, just like when I got out of David's truck. She went on and on, they were deliberating between a hotel and a beach house, she wanted to ask my advice on which car to rent and where to go touring. I held the phone at arm's length, and when she went quiet, I returned the phone to my ear and told her it all sounded wonderful and promised to check out the possibility of taking a two-week vacation, I might even be able to join them in Greece and make it to Israel for a short visit.

"It's been ages since we went on vacation together," she reproached me, and we hung up.

2

The fifteenth time I went shooting in America, I was alone. It was a Sunday, the day after I'd gone out with the others and my finger froze on the trigger. I didn't think I would go out hunting on my own again, not after what happened to me that past winter. But something made me go, regardless. I needed to understand what happened back there, why I'd been unable to shoot.

Later that week I had a busy business trip scheduled. David and I were going together. Two big clients, three flights in three days, two hotels.

The rifle was already loaded, I'd seen to that after parking the car, before I entered the grounds. "A loaded gun," I said out loud to ensure I didn't get it wrong again.

All was quiet as I walked along, and soon enough I reached what looked like a good observation point. I went down on bended knees and stayed like that until my knees started to hurt, and then

I lay down on the ground. Quite some time went by until I saw them approaching. There were two, one smaller than the other. I inhaled deeply and then exhaled, emptying my lungs. I saw them clearly through the gunsight, they stood there, motionless. My finger froze on the trigger guard, pushing down hard on the metal. My eyes flickered above the gunsight and I lost focus. I closed my eyes and opened them again, I tried to concentrate. This time I succeeded, and I aimed the rifle at the same spot. They were still standing there. I focused on the bigger one, but there was something strange there, it took me a while to figure out that the animal had lost its buck head. The big animal stood there, head held high, it was a human head. I shifted the rifle in the direction of the smaller animal, grazing on forage. When she suddenly raised her head and set her gaze on me, I saw she had a human head as well. I panicked and fired two shots. First one shot, a quick charge, and then a second one. I wasn't sure I had hit anything. But I saw the large one fleeing. I lay there a little longer.

When I stood over the small animal, its human head had disappeared completely. It lay there motionless with its deer head. Something inside me did not want to leave the fawn there. I tried dragging it back to the car, but it was impossible. I didn't stand a chance; it was way too heavy. I left it there in the middle of the trail. On my way back to the car, I saw a beautiful big flower, bright purple in color. I picked it and retraced my steps. When I reached the animal, I placed the flower on its body. I lingered there, staring at it.

3

On Monday, at work, a colleague asked me if I was okay. "I just wondered if you need anything," she said. I stared at her, a little surprised, and then I came to my senses and said I was fine, that it was just the change in seasons, and I added jokingly that I wasn't used to so many seasons. "Thanks for your concern, that's so nice of you," I said and flashed her my new smile, keeping it broad and big until she smiled too and went back to her office.

It felt weird that someone would make such a remark, particularly someone who was not close to me. But she was right, it was obvious I was wasting away. My body was constantly shrinking, my flesh contracting into itself. When I first noticed I was losing weight, I thought it was the cold. That first winter in America had been the coldest I'd ever experienced. But the weight loss did not cease when winter was over. Following the wave of layoffs at work and the hunting trips at the vacation home, my appetite had utterly disappeared.

After she left, I closed the door and didn't leave my office the entire day. I preferred to be alone, I had a lot of work to do before my trip with David. Meanwhile, I was still troubled by that little animal.

4

David picked me up before the flight, arriving promptly at four in the morning, as promised. He was leaning against his truck as I exited the house, waiting to put my case inside it.

The flight left on schedule and passed uneventfully. My laptop was open the entire way as I went over material for our upcoming meeting. At the airport we picked up the rental car that the company reserved for us. We had our first meeting with a client later that morning. David drove, and I switched on the laptop so we could run through the key points before our first meeting. After traveling for an hour, David exited the highway, and we stopped at a restaurant by a service station. I ordered coffee and pancakes with a mountain of whipped cream topped with a purply sauce that had once been blueberries. There was no proportion between my appetite and the amount of food I ordered. I ate listlessly, and after a few bites I pushed the plate to the other side of the table. I went to freshen up in the restroom, and when I washed my face with water I closed my eyes so as not to see myself in the mirror.

We were a little early for our meeting. We waited at the reception desk while they issued us temporary entry permits, as though we were at a border crossing. It was not much different from our other clients, most companies had visitors sign a short-term agreement, like a confidentiality statement, before entering the premises.

A few minutes after they called from the reception desk, our escort arrived. He looked as if he'd run all the way from the building to the path and from there to reception. His cheeks were flushed, and he was panting, a bulky, red-haired guy. We walked behind him along the path to the second floor of the company's central offices. On the entrance sign beside the company's initials it said: MAIN CAMPUS.

The escort took us into the conference room and then left. Through the glass wall I watched him walking off with quick steps into the open space, until he vanished. A few minutes later a woman came in with a tray of refreshments, a pot of coffee, and milk, and then returned with a pot of tea.

David got up and offered me coffee, I gestured to go ahead and pour me some. Meanwhile, I switched on my laptop but didn't connect to the Wi-Fi with the username and password they'd assigned us. Instead, I got online with the chip the IT guy at the office gave me before we left on Monday. He cautioned me that there was a risk, albeit low, that operators at clients' sites were running espionage programs. A small chuckle escaped me. David didn't notice.

Shortly before the meeting was scheduled to begin, three people entered the conference room: the guy who escorted us from the reception desk, and two others.

5

After a few minutes of small talk, the meeting began. David and I sat on one side of the table, the other three sat opposite us. To the left sat Hugh, the red-haired guy. He was the client's project manager. To his left sat Keenan, the maintenance manager, and Chris, a junior engineer who was working exclusively on this project. Hugh, Keenan, and Chris, Hugh, Keenan, and Chris, I repeated their names in my head several times. The meeting lasted six hours, with several coffee breaks at intervals. We didn't leave the conference room until a little after six in the evening. The first part of the meeting passed quite quickly, we went through the first section in the requirements document and agreed on most of the amendments. During the next break, the woman who had brought coffee returned with two trays of sandwiches. I didn't touch the food, but whenever my coffee cup emptied, I gestured for David to refill it. Sometimes he refilled it on his own initiative. In the second part of the meeting, we went over the main section of the requirements document. It was more detailed, and we examined the technical aspects in depth, which required concentration. Toward the end of the meeting, I noticed my phone was dying, only a few percent remained. I reached down to grab my bag. When I lifted my head, I almost hit it on the table. I connected the cable to the laptop and then to the in-table power socket. David said something and one of them answered, I wasn't sure who. My thoughts wandered and the voices in the room floated above me, I no longer understood what they were saying. When I lifted my gaze from the screen of my laptop for a moment I saw only the animal. She was lying there, halfway along the trail. The purple flower was not there, which troubled me. When did it disappear, there was no way she ate it, she wasn't alive. A moment later I felt David's hand on my back. "Did you enter Chris's last comment?" he asked. I turned my attention back to the screen and typed in the last comment, which somehow had registered in my brain, lodged itself somewhere in the back of my mind. I didn't see her after that, she vanished, it was Chris who was sitting across the table from me. David poured me some more coffee, and after a brief discussion in which I presented some of the project's constraints, I added some final remarks to the document, and we moved on to the summarization stage. David summarized the meeting on his laptop, typing slowly with one finger in his characteristic way, occasionally lifting his eyes to the screen to make sure the cursor had not jumped and was still in the right place.

6

On our way out, David patted me on the back again and asked if I was okay. He said I looked a bit out of it toward the end of the meeting.

"The flight tired me out," I responded dismissively.

We drove for a few hours to a different airport. David concentrated on driving and occasionally switched radio channels. After a while, he asked again: "Are you sure you're feeling okay? You look a bit pale."

"The ride's making me nauseous, that's all."

At the airport, after returning the rental car, entering the terminal, and making our way to the boarding gate, I went into the restroom. I turned on the faucet and washed my face with warm water. This time I didn't avoid the mirror. I was extremely pale. I took out moisturizer from my bag and applied it carefully, rubbing my cheeks, gradually my face looked less gray. I ran my fingers through my hair and fixed it. I applied some lipstick, changed my mind, and wiped it off with water and toilet paper.

David was waiting for me in the seating area by the boarding gate. He looked at me strangely as I approached, as if he didn't recognize me. On a small table between our seats were two cups of coffee and two small sandwiches. "Choose whichever you want, I wasn't sure which you'd prefer." When I asked him how Miriam was, he didn't reply, and then there was an announcement, and our names were called out. They called David's name and then mine, the pronunciation of my name completely distorted. If my name hadn't been called right after David's, I wouldn't have recognized it. We approached the counter, David exchanged a few words with the agent, and we made our way to the other side of the seating area, reserved for first class and business passengers.

7

The plane was bigger than I expected.

Business class was almost empty. Aside from David and me, there were only two or three others seated a few rows behind us. David sat on the other side of the aisle, and I beckoned him to come sit next to me. The flight attendant passed through with newspapers, and David took one. The pilot announced we would be taking off soon, the screens lit up, and the preflight safety video began.

The flight attendant passed through the cabin as soon as the FASTEN SEAT BELT sign went off. She offered soft drinks and handed us the wine menu. I chose one of the red wines and went to the restroom. By the time I got back to my seat, the drinks had arrived along with the dinner menu. I sipped the wine and reclined my seat as close to lying flat as possible. I woke up just before the plane landed. When I opened my eyes, David was looking at me. "We're landing any minute," he said.

It took me a few seconds to realize I was holding something in my hand: It was David's hand, and it was warm. Our fingers were intertwined. I released my hold and returned my seat to an upright position. Shortly after, the plane landed on the runway. A soft landing, I barely felt the impact of the wheels on the tarmac.

8

We got to the hotel late that night. I fell asleep on the bed immediately, without taking off the covers or changing my clothes, I didn't even remove my shoes. In the morning, awoken by the alarm clock, I felt as though I'd hardly slept. Despite taking a warm shower, I could not shake off my exhaustion.

At seven in the morning, we met for breakfast. At a quarter to nine, we were already standing in front of a guard at the entrance to the offices of our second client. The guard called our escort, then photographed us and issued entry permits printed on stickers with an embedded barcode. When our escort arrived, the guard asked us to go through the metal detector. We scanned the code on the stickers and the device beeped like a check-out machine in a supermarket. Finally, a green light came on and we walked through.

It was a spacious conference room, with a large table at the center and beyond it a glass wall of windows overlooking the greenery outside, the actual world beyond the company grounds. I sat facing the windows and David sat down next to me; our hosts sat opposite us, their backs to the windows.

A few minutes later, an elderly woman entered the room and set bottles of soft drinks and glasses on the table. She returned several times with various refreshments, cookies, fruit, a coffeepot, a teapot and cups, back and forth until the table was set. David poured coffee for me, and then for himself. I reached out and took an apple from the fruit platter.

A few minutes before the meeting was scheduled to begin, a man and a woman entered the room, and we shook hands. They introduced themselves and then screened a presentation showcasing their company. They spoke with more pronounced Southern accents than the clients from the previous day. I forgot their names immediately, and since they insisted on calling me *Miss* and David *Sir*, I called them that too. The meeting was successful and much shorter than the previous one, under two hours. It was an introductory meeting to manage expectations without getting into the specifics of the upcoming project. On my way out, I glanced at the temporary entry tag I'd been issued. The low quality of the photo perfectly captured the gray shade of my skin.

We were given a brief tour after the meeting. They took us to the proposed site for the desalination plant we were planning for them. We shared some basic ideas, I opened my notepad and took notes. The ink leaked onto the page, staining my fingers. On the way back, one of our hosts offered to take us on a tour of the factory. David thanked him and said we'd be happy to tour the factory some other time.

9

It was only when we turned onto the access road leading to the airport that I recognized where we were. I'd had a layover at this very airport last year. David heard me chuckling to myself and asked me what was so funny. "Nothing," I said, "just a dumb thought passing through my head." When we entered the rental company's parking lot, David asked me what my plans were for the weekend. I told him I was thinking of flying to New York. I hadn't a clue where that idea came from, it popped into my head as I was talking. Somehow, I managed to convince myself this had been my plan all along. I told him I had a good friend in New York with whom I could stay. David looked at me in surprise but said nothing. The truth is, I hadn't been in touch with this friend at all. We were close friends when I was living in Israel, but when I moved to the US it actually distanced us, each of us on separate sides of the continent. We wrote each other for a while, but by winter we had stopped.

When we entered the terminal, we discovered that David's flight was delayed by two hours. He insisted on coming with me to the airline counter. I bought a ticket to New York and another one back home. The agent agreed to lower the price of the return ticket after David pulled out his membership card. He was a platinum member or perhaps something even higher than that, the kind of level he could never descend from, even if he tried. She found me a standby ticket and warned me I may not be able to get on the next flight, I should watch the board to check for priority boarding. She said that all the flights were fully booked and there were ten people ahead of me on the waiting list. I didn't care, I already knew where I was headed. David had another hour before his flight back. I went with him to the boarding gate, and when we said goodbye, he squeezed my hand and said it had been a productive trip. It was true, we accomplished a lot, the clients seemed satisfied, but somehow it wasn't enough, nothing was enough anymore. I stepped toward him and gave him a hug, at first it was a limp hug but it intensified into a tight embrace.

After we parted I went to the business lounge. I remembered it was somewhere around there, and it really was—I recognized the sleeping pods from far away. After a few minutes I found pod number two, it was vacant. When I swiped my card the door opened, just like the first time. A moment before lying down on the bed, I removed the cell phone from my bag. It was late in Israel. I typed a quick text message.

Mom, I'm checking to see if I can join you in Greece
Send me the details
Love to Dad too

10

I set the phone to silent mode and pulled down the roller blind until it clicked. Everything was exactly as I recalled. I removed my shoes and my socks, I took off my jacket, shirt, and pants. I remained in my underwear and a thin undershirt. After a few moments, I got out of bed and switched on the light so I could take out the earplugs from my bag. Once they were snugly in my ears, I finally achieved peace and quiet. I glanced at the screen of my phone before placing it in my bag and a text message popped up. It was from David.

I'm boarding now
Enjoy NY

I adjusted the air-conditioning. I wanted it to be just right. I peeked through the curtain but couldn't see anyone outside the pod, so I switched off the light. The blanket was taut across the bed, like in a hotel. I felt perfectly snug and safe. At first I lay on my side. Then I turned over and lay on my back. It was not long before I fell asleep.

11

I got to the departure gate in time to see the jet-way pulling away from the plane. Everything moved clumsily, in slow motion. My name was flashing across the screen in red letters, I'd missed my place on the standby list. Maybe if I'd hurried, I would have made it, maybe if I'd skipped watching the pod go through its routine, I would have got there in time. I checked my phone. There were no new messages, not even from my mom, which seemed odd after the message I sent her. It was already morning in Israel. When I scrolled through our conversation on my phone, I saw that the message had been typed but not sent—I must have forgotten to press send. Instead of sending it now, I deleted it.

The plane landed at dawn. While waiting for my baggage to arrive I wondered if I should take a taxi. In the end I called David. I told myself I'd let the phone ring two or three times and then hang up if he didn't answer, but he picked up after one ring, as if he'd been sitting there all this time, waiting for me to call. "I need you to come pick me up from the airport," I said.

When he pulled up to my house, there was heavy fog. We remained sitting in the car. When I finally got out of the car I told him to come in. I entered the house, left my case by the door, and went straight upstairs. David followed me. This was the first time he had ever walked through my front door, the first time he had crossed over the threshold. I took a shower and David stayed in the bedroom. When I came out of the shower he was sitting on the bed, waiting for me. I asked if he was going into work that morning and he said no. Months had passed since our brief stay in the vacation home. We never talked about what happened, not since that evening in the restaurant, when I returned David's keys. I threw myself into work, the same way I threw myself into work after Eran. I was in a new position. My actual role had barely changed but my status had. He was effectively my manager, although we avoided defining it as such. When he presented the new organizational structure to the department, my name appeared in a little box floating to the right of his name, the upper border of the box was only slightly lower than the upper border of the box containing his name. The job title did not change, it remained senior project manager, and David oversaw the entire department. During these months, David had distanced himself from me, or perhaps I withdrew from him.

When David got into bed with me that morning, it felt as though everything happened by chance. In a split-second decision I called him, he answered just like that, and then he decided not to go to work, and stayed at my place. When I moved on top of him, his eyes were wide-open, looking at me the same way he had looked at me back in the hotel bathroom. This time, however, it was closer, as if it were from the inside. When I awoke a few hours later, David was still lying there in bed, next to me.

12

David stayed a few weeks, then a few months. The days flowed into each other and merged, they lost their edges and were welded together into a single entity. He woke up very early every morning while I was still deep in sleep. He left no belongings in the bedroom, the room retained no trace of him. Every morning he packed the few belongings he had brought with him the night before: his clothes, his laptop, toiletries. Coffee was ready in the kitchen, kept warm in a pot on the stand of the coffee maker, practically the only evidence that David had been with me. Before, I never used the coffee machine, it all seemed like too much trouble for me, I preferred to leave early and either drink my first coffee at work or pick up one on my way there. By the time I got to the office at around eight in the morning, David was already there, dressed in clean clothes, freshly shaven. We made a point of only talking about work-related issues in the office. At my place, on the other hand, we hardly ever talked about work. Over dinner, David asked me about Israel, my family, places I'd lived in. I told him about my childhood home, about the four-story building with the elevator. I told him about the spacious apartment we later moved to, in a nicer part of town. I tried to count all the Tel Aviv apartments I had lived in but I got stuck. I was sure I was missing one of them, maybe more than one. David was amazed there were so many but what amazed him even more was how small they had been compared to the vast house in which I now lived. David said he'd only lived in two houses his entire life, with a short break between them. Nineteen years living at home with his parents, a break during college when he lived in the dorms, and then a little over thirty years in the house he and Miriam owned.

In the conference rooms at work, we always sat in the same places, next to each other; in the cafeteria we sat at separate tables, as we had always done. By tacit agreement, we continued as usual, with no signs of either particular closeness, or distance. We had sex almost every night, but now it felt different. I didn't put a label on it, I just knew I would see him every night. Without saying anything, David came back every single night; I got used to his presence, to our conversations over dinner, to his body in my bed.

Every day at closing time, he swung by my office and said goodbye, sometimes he said, "See you," or "Goodbye now." I heard him repeat those same words over and over to other employees in adjacent offices, until his voice faded and he disappeared down the hallway and out into the parking lot.

13

On my return home from work, the house was always empty. David arrived later. I didn't ask where he'd been or what he'd done between leaving the office and appearing on my doorstep. He always rang the doorbell, he never entered without an invitation, although the door was open. Sometimes, in the hours before bedtime, we each did our own thing. We usually ate dinner together and sometimes David picked up something for us to eat. The weather turned warmer, but we didn't go out hunting during those weeks. David didn't suggest it, and neither did I. I assumed it was the changing seasons. Deer season was over, and pheasant season was about to begin.

One evening, just after we sat down for dinner, David told me that Miriam had left him. "She decided she'd had enough," he said dryly, without telling me when it happened or going into any other details. When I asked him how he felt, he said it really didn't matter, they had left each other long ago. He never used the word *separation* when talking about Miriam, not then, and not ever. He did not tell me where she went, or what happened to all her belongings, or the house. While we were eating, he suddenly said that at first she was apprehensive about motherhood, and he feared for her, but his fear turned to admiration when he saw how devoted she was to Tom. "Tom was her greatest love," he said, her love for him was enormous. He told me that in the first few years of their marriage she didn't want children at all, even when her friends and her sister became mothers. She was 100 percent dedicated to the school where she taught, and hoped to make time for writing. She read everything she could get her hands on, books from the public library and secondhand books sent to her in the mail. When she was a few weeks pregnant, she informed him that she had no intention of quitting her job and that he should start planning an extended leave of absence from work. In the end they both took six months, and it was the best time they ever had together, when they were a family. David said that people around him didn't know what to make of it, they had never heard of a man taking paternity leave. It was only after the accident that everyone agreed it had been a smart idea, at least they'd been fortunate enough to have had that time together.

14

A **few weeks went by, and he did not mention** Miriam again. It was pleasant outside, and we began to talk about hunting again. The pheasant season had begun. Occasionally David said it was a pity to miss it, but a week passed and another one and we did not find the time. Work was more intensive than ever, and there were days of back-to-back meetings, with no breaks between them. David was absent a lot, his business trips became more frequent, sometimes he went away for a couple of days, sometimes five. Between business trips he would show up at my house in the middle of the night, I left the door unlocked for him. In the morning I would wake up and find him gone. I would go downstairs and coffee would be waiting for me in the kitchen. I knew he'd probably fallen asleep on the couch. It was around that time I noticed my period was late. This was unusual, but since we had barely seen each other for the past few weeks, I decided it was nothing. I did the first pregnancy test after a week, I was sure it would be negative. I was relieved when it came out negative, but another week passed and I still did not get my period. I did another test, and that one was negative too. When my period was two weeks late, I made an appointment with a gynecologist. I hoped that by the time my appointment came, my period would have arrived and there would be no reason to go to her and if I did, it would only be for a routine checkup. I didn't tell David, he was away on another business trip. Even when he returned, I said nothing. I didn't want to tell him before I was completely sure. He landed in the morning and went straight to work. When I saw him by the coffee machine, he was talking to one of the engineers. He nodded hello in my direction. I went back to my office, expecting him to come by, but he didn't. In the evening he turned up at my place, carrying a bottle of wine and some groceries to make dinner.

That night he fell into a deep sleep before me. I heard his shallow, short breath rising and falling. The bedside lamp on his side was on, and I watched his shadow rise and fall on the wall opposite. He mumbled in his sleep and turned over to the other side, his back to me. I got out of bed to switch off the lamp, and I heard him mumbling again. As I bent down, I heard the words, "I'm asking you, please, please." I switched off the lamp and the room went quiet. Then I heard his breath again, rising and falling, a measured, quiet whistling.

15

The last time I went hunting in America was sometime after that. Spring was almost over, and we went out just the two of us. The pheasant season was drawing to a close, David said the bag limit was two birds per licensed hunter through the end of the season. He said we could each shoot one bird. Even at the end of that first year I was still not a licensed hunter. David split his quota with me. We set out with only one rifle between us, I didn't ask David why he brought only one. Meanwhile, I made it to the appointment with the gynecologist. David was preparing himself for an important board meeting and we barely had the chance to meet. At work and at my place too we smiled as we passed each other, communicating with our usual code. The coffee on the kitchen table, the door left unlocked at night, the same seats around the conference table at work. Some mornings I had trouble figuring out whether David had slept in my bed or not.

When we went out hunting for the last time, David had just returned from another business trip, and we hadn't slept together for several nights. I preferred it that way, I still wasn't sure what was going on with me, what to decide about the pregnancy. I kept it to myself and told no one. David shot first and missed; the birds flew away screeching. He was sullen, and it reminded me of his behavior at the vacation home, during the storm, when Miriam called.

She had disappeared completely. He did not utter her name even once throughout those last weeks of spring, not since the night he mumbled in his sleep and I thought perhaps I heard her name. I didn't ask about her again. As if she had been erased from the face of the earth. I had no idea where she'd gone, I presumed to her sister's. There were moments I doubted she even existed, even though I had met her, even though we had talked. Sometimes I thought perhaps it was David who had left over the winter, and she who had stayed at home.

In fact, once he almost said her name. It was on one of his business trips. He called asking for updates on some project or other, usually I gave him the same answer, according to the status that appeared in the system or that had been emailed. He always ended the conversation the same way, "Great, see you soon, goodbye now," in a kind of purposeful, automatic managerial tone. And then something went south, and he blurted out his nickname for Miriam, "See you soon, Mir." He came to his senses and said he had to hang up, he had a waiting call. Then he hung up.

One time when David was away, I drove to their house. I didn't plan it in advance. The car took me there one day on my way to work. All the windows were shuttered, and Miriam's car wasn't parked in the driveway where it usually stood. I peeked into the garage, and it wasn't there either.

X

The last time I went hunting in America I hit the target with my first bullet. After I shot it, the bird fell to the ground very quickly. It took me by surprise, although I was familiar with the laws of physics. It was a lovely day and the sky was clear. Blue the way blue could be imagined, an unbelievable blue I had only ever seen in America.

I had taken my shot after David's failed one. He handed me the rifle and we continued walking along. A flock of pheasants flew in the distance. As they drew closer, David grabbed my arm and said, "Take your time, wait until they're nearer." His hand held my arm tightly, he was hurting me, but I didn't say anything. After he released his grip, I aimed at the bird from a standing position and released a bullet. The echoing sound of the bullet joined the birds' screeching, and there was a thud as the bird fell to the ground.

It took a while before we saw the flock from afar, I think it was David who saw it first. His right hand shielded his eyes from the sun, he pointed and said, "Here, see, it looks like they're heading in our direction." There was a moment when they seemed to be gliding away in murmuration, but then they turned toward us, as though they were dancing. After the shot I heard David in the background, still talking, a medley of words I couldn't understand, my head was troubled by the thud on the ground, by the bird.

On the morning of the last time I went hunting in America I sent David a text message. I asked when he was coming, but he didn't answer. All the while I had a bad feeling, but I didn't think it would be the last time. When he came to pick me up, he waited outside. He didn't call to tell me I should come out to the car, nor did he come to the door. I saw him from the window of the bedroom while I was getting dressed to go out. He stood by the car, his eyes shielded by sunglasses, his face turned to the front door, waiting.

After I shot the bird, I handed the rifle to David and began running to where it fell, the air was so clean. After a few moments I turned around, but I couldn't see him. I thought maybe he was running alongside me, or maybe aiming the rifle at another flock gliding in the opposite direction, I could hear the birds. I kept running with the sense that a little bit more and the air would lift me away, upward, like in a dream. A few steps before

I reached the pheasant, I turned around again, this time I saw him clearly. David was standing straight, a distance away from me. Suddenly he seemed much older than he looked close up, standing or sitting next to me. The light sparkled on his sunglasses, resting atop his mane of gray hair, his elbow parallel to the ground and the rifle we shared that day aimed directly at me. For a moment I imagined Miriam, flickering behind him, holding the binoculars, double-checking, wanting to know if there was any life left in the animal lying there.

Acknowledgments

Thank you to my love, Tomer Haruv, to my sister, Efrat Hakimi, to Oded Wolkstein, for the friendship and our conversations, to Joanna Chen, for her brilliant translation work, to my agent, Geula Geurts, at the Deborah Harris Agency, for making this happen, to my editor, Camille LeBlanc, for believing in this book, and to Naama Tsal, for all she taught me.